I0735683

Campfires and Complications

Georgianna Lockman

Copyright © 2025 by Georgianna Lockman

All rights reserved.

No portion of this book may be reproduced in any form without written permission from the publisher or author, except as permitted by U.S. copyright law.

Contents

Chapter 1

My head is pounding. It feels like there are a thousand hammering drums in my head that will never end. My throat is parched and every time I try to swallow it's like I'm eating sandpaper. It's not the hefty fire that crackles and pops ominously before me or the weird shrieking noise that's getting louder and closer with each passing second or even the fact that my once long black hair that fell to my elbows has been cut so it now barely brushes past my jawline. No, the thing that catches my attention first and foremost is the fact that my back is against a pole and my arms and legs have been tied securely to it with a rope.

"Peryn," says a raspy voice belonging to my best friend.

I look over at her, her once long blonde hair has been hacked away too, leaving a badly cut bob and like me she's been tied to a long metal pole.

"Hi, Per," she stares at me with wide eyes, "Can...you...Can you hear the birds singing?"

"Are you still hopped up on those berries?" I ask, she giggles and I frown.

"Oh wow, the night is...so pretty," she giggles again, her head swaying a little.

She's tied between her brother and his best friend who've also been fixed to the poles. They're both unconscious, I start praying for them to wake up soon.

"Wait," she says all starry-eyed, "can you see them?"

"See what?"

"The fairies," she whispers, "they're so pretty!"

Fear has fully settled in, clawing away at me as I see the dark figures of our captors coming closer and closer. How the hell did this happen? This was supposed to be a pleasant and peaceful camping trip. We were supposed to be spending five days camping in the wilds surrounded by nature, not five days of running for our lives from a crazy bear, rabid wolves and almost dying in a lake. How did it turn into such a horror fest? I'm exhausted, I'm hungry, my clothes are ripped and dirty, I have bruises in places I didn't even know you could get bruises, I haven't slept for forty-eight hours, and I'm pretty sure that angry bear is still stalking us.

"Oh my God," I breathe, frantically trying to undo the ropes but no matter how I hard I try they won't come off. It's no use, they've really knotted it tightly. It's beginning to cut the circulation in my hands and legs.

The sound of footsteps approaching pulls me out of my thoughts. The flickering light of the fire makes the duo look even more sinister. They step into the light of the fire and my jaw drops when I realise who the creepy pair are.

"You!" I gasp as I stare wide eyed at them, "you bastards!"

The pair are wearing long white robes and a lot of wooden jewelry. I take in the long sticks they're carrying, the hats that look like – what I hope aren't real – deer skulls and the white swirling lines drawn onto their faces. This should bother me, this should really worry me but I've seen and done so many weird things these past few days that nothing seems to faze me anymore. This, I realize with horror, has become normality.

"What the hell is wrong with you people?" I ask, "You need help! Who does this?"

"Be quiet!" She snaps.

"This evening!" The short, chubby man screeches as he raises the stick in the air, "this evening your bodies and souls shall be sacrificed to the great moon spirit above!"

I'm starting to think that maybe this camping trip was a bad idea after all.

Chapter 2

6 DAYS AGO

Vancouver, Canada

"Jude has herpes."

I looked up from the menu I'd been scanning. "Huh?"

"Jude has herpes," she repeated.

"Ew, what?"

"Jude has herpes," she said monotonously.

I stared at her, my expression was somewhere between disgust and shock, "Oh my God, how the hell–"

Callie sputtered and suddenly burst out laughing. She threw her head back, snorts mingled with her cackling laughter. I warily glanced around the cafe. People had turned their heads and were looking over at us. Her howl-like laughter was quickly catching the attention of the entire cafe. One of the waitresses behind the counter was glaring unhappily. If Callie didn't shut up she would get us kicked out. I smiled sheepishly, offering the woman some reassurance and turned back to my best friend. I kicked her leg from underneath the table.

"Ow!" she cried, her laughter instantly died.

"Callie," I hissed, "you'll get us kicked out."

"S'okay," she said and waved her hand dismissively, "I know the owner, we're fine."

Even though the owner of the café, a stern frizzy-haired woman from Ottawa, was a close friend of Callie's family, it didn't mean she wouldn't kick us out. She'd threatened to do just that more times than I would like and it was all because of Callie.

She was too loud and she didn't know how to be discreet. Okay, I was loud too but it wasn't too point where the café would fall silent like they did with Callie. Honestly, I was surprised we hadn't been banned from the café sooner. We were a little obnoxious. I hoped we never would. I don't know where else we would go, Lemon & Lime was the only decent café this side of Vancouver.

"Why did you say Jude has herpes?" I asked, striking the straw into the lid of my drink.

She smiled, "I need a believable rumour to spread about that asshole."

"Ah," I nodded my head slowly in understanding. I popped the straw into my mouth and took a long sip of my mango smoothie. I shrugged and said, "It's believable, he is a whore."

Last week Callie had split with her boyfriend of nine months, Jude Sinclair. I wasn't really surprised, Jude and Callie had this exasperating on and off relationship that no one could really keep up with. If it weren't for Ethan Rosenberg and Santiago Garcia, Jude and Callie would be the golden couple at James Wolfe School. Callie was really bitter about it. She never understood what everybody thought was so special about Ethan and Santiago.

She liked them fine, she was even the one who got them together, she just didn't like the fact they were a more popular couple. I didn't tell her I disagreed because if you saw Ethan Rosenberg and Santiago Garcia, who were crazy hot, you would instantly understand why everybody loved them so much. I also didn't tell her I never understood what she saw in Jude Sinclair. Sure, he was handsome, the captain of the varsity baseball team and one of the most popular boys at our high school but he was shallow and promiscuous and really slimy.

Callie let out a long sigh and took a bite from her hamburger, "I miss him."

It was ridiculous. They only got back together a month ago and just last Thursday, Callie had dragged me into the bathroom and told me she'd ended things with Jude. I'd seen the break up coming from a mile away.

It was a well-known fact Jude Sinclair was a vain douchebag. Not that anyone had the guts to say it to his face. Well, not since he'd tackled Oliver Kaminski to the ground in ninth grade for saying his hair was like an old woman's. Big mistake. Everyone knew Jude Sinclair loved his hair. Hey, that rhymed.

"Now, I know what you're thinking," Callie said through a mouthful of hamburger, "Jude is a dick and I totally deserve better, but Per, me and Jude totally work."

"Last week you threw a ketchup bottle at his face in front of everyone in the cafeteria," I said. That was the day after Callie broke up with Jude and found out from Reinette Thayer that he'd kissed a cheerleader from a neighbouring high school. "If I remember correctly you called him the c-word, threatened to him have hanged and then you declared to whole the cafeteria how you two totally don't work and never will."

It was a horrifying moment but at the same time it was the best thing that had happened all month. Jude's scream when the ketchup bottle his face was a sound I wish I could have recorded and made into my ringtone. Callie Marshall and her meltdowns were a huge source of entertainment for me and the population of James Wolfe School.

I'd warned Callie about Jude, but as usual, she chose to ignore me. When Callie broke up with him, she liked to go through vast volumes of mint chocolate chip ice cream and re-watch Titanic. I hid any sharp and heavy objects because she liked to throw things. This usually lasted for about a week or two before she got back together with Jude.

"You know what?" she said, taking another a bite from her hamburger, "Jude Sinclair can go die in a hole, I am so fucking done with boys."

I fought the urge to roll my eyes. I swear, if I had a dollar for every time Callie said this. I just didn't understand why Callie couldn't find a decent guy. She was beautiful and kind and admittedly a little bit of an airhead but she had a good heart.

"Is that so?" I said dryly. I swirled the straw round for a few seconds before slurping in the sweet and icy liquid.

It was like any other Saturday afternoon. Callie and I were sat in one of the booths at the back of the café. It was a good spot, right next to the vending machine and the jukebox.

"Only two days into spring break and I'm already bored out of my mind," Callie said.

I sighed, "Me too."

Callie placed the hamburger down. I was tempted to ask if I could have some but I knew Callie was really protective of her food. She didn't share with anyone. Even if that someone was a starving best friend who had gone grown tired of her smoothie.

I hummed, "are you sure Mrs. Brames said no cheer practice this week?"

She stared at me, "it's spring break Per, when have we ever had cheer practice during spring break?"

I pouted. It was stupid question and I knew she was right but I was hoping otherwise. If there was one thing I didn't hate about James Wolfe – and there was a lot I hated about that school– it was the cheer squad. I joined at the start of high school because my mom was pressuring me to do an afterschool sport.

This was only because she'd watched an episode of The Biggest Loser and was terrified that I would end up on that show. She'd said the last thing needed in her life was another obese child to worry about. It was either lacrosse or cheerleading and since lacrosse looked really weird and complicated, I went with cheerleading. Callie joined me on the team a few weeks later. It turned out to be the best thing at school and I couldn't imagine what my life would look like without it.

"I don't want cheer practice anyway," Callie said, "I nearly broke my leg last time thanks to Ammara Ali. Why is she even on the team? She is the most uncoordinated person I have ever seen. Mark my words someone is going to die because of her."

"You're being dramatic, she's a good gymnast and she's not uncoordinated," I said as I stole a few fries from her plate and shoved them in my mouth, "you just don't like her because she dated Jude that one time in ninth grade."

"Whatever," she grumbled.

I used to think that cheerleading was for airheads but I was so wrong. It was hard and it required so much work. I'd sprained a few bones but it was worth it to get that thrill of adrenaline after a performance and a major positive of cheerleading was that you got the pick of hottest guys at school.

"You know what we should do?" Callie said, her cornflower blue eyes lit up.

"What?"

"Camping!" she beamed at me, "we should go camping!"

"What? Camping?" I said, "Callie, you hate camping."

"Per," she placed both arms on the table and leaned forward, her smile was bright, "it'll be fun. We have two weeks off for spring break. We need to do something. Think about it, me, you, nature, and birds...and shit and I really need to get my mind off Jude. Please. Please?"

It actually wasn't a bad idea. I had always loved camping. My dad and I used to do it every summer when I was kid. Some of my best memories were spent huddled around the campfire exchanging light stories with my parents and my sisters. I hadn't been in so long I had forgotten what it was like.

Also, I thought, it would be a great opportunity to get away from my mom and her obsessive behavior over the wedding. Two months ago my parents had decided to renew the vows for their twentieth wedding anniversary. Don't get me wrong, I was happy for them, ecstatic actually but Mom had gotten really neurotic in the past few weeks and she was annoying the hell out of me. I needed a break from her before I said something I regretted or she did something she regretted, like hiring that Bee Gees tribute band Dad wanted.

I grinned at Callie, "Sure! Why not?"

Chapter 3

The whole reason my parents were even getting their vows renewed was because Mom saw this segment on The Marilyn Denis Show about Drew Barrymore's wedding and how it was this simple and traditional ceremony that happened over a weekend with close friends and family and how it was probably the most talked about wedding of the year. The fact it made it onto the cover of People magazine only made my mom squeal louder.

She spent two straight days reading about the wedding, who was there, what did the venue look like, her wedding dress. My youngest sister made the mistake of asking Mom what her wedding was like and Mom got really emotional and took out the photo album. I was dragged into it and I had to sit for two hours as Mom guided me and Dione through every picture and the story behind it.

Three days later, Callie came over to my house and we were both re-watching the fifth season of America's Next Top Model, when Mom barged into the living room and declared she was getting married. To Dad. Again. She said they were getting their vows renewed because it was romantic and it was going to be way better than Drew Barrymore's ever was.

I love the romance, the fact two people were agreeing to spend the rest of their lives to together in front of their family and friends was the most romantic thing ever. I always ended up crying during the wedding ceremony, usually around the time the bride and groom were declared man and wife. I loved seeing what the bride was wearing, my sisters and I would usually judge and rate their dress.

Not to mention seeing the venue, and the food and especially the cake. It was a really emotional event for me and I loved every aspect of it. So when Mom said they would be renewing their vows it was the best thing I had heard all year. So the next two months I helped plan the wedding and it was really fun choosing what dress she was going to wear and the food and who was invited and best of all, I got to spend some quality with my mom.

As much as I enjoyed planning this wedding with her, Mom was starting to get on my nerves. It was early April and the wedding was next month, on the second week of May and the closer it was, the more neurotic and just downright annoying my mom became. This camping trip Callie had suggested was a blessing. It would be great to have a break from the wedding plans.

After I came home from Lemon & Lime with Callie, I told Mom I was going camping. Actually, I waited until she was in a better mood and then I told her. I expected I would have to convince her and I had my argument all ready. My argument was mainly comprised of the fact I was sixteen and I would be entering the twelfth grade after the summer. To my surprise, when I told Mom of my plans to go camping with Callie, she smiled and said it was fine. Apparently I deserved a little break after all the help I had given her with the wedding.

When, Tuesday afternoon rolled around, the day we'd decided to go camping, I was in my bedroom collecting the last of my things. Everybody was okay with me going, it was just my little sister who had a problem. Dione had been pestering me ever since she found out.

"No!" she said, "you can't go!"

"Calm down," I told her, "it'll only be for a few days."

Dione pouted, "that's too long! I need you here!"

"For what?"

She threw her arms in the air, "Stuff!"

I laughed, "You know Di, as exciting as stuff sounds, I still need to go."

She folded her arms across her chest and she huffed. I set my rucksack on the edge of the bed and placing my hands on her shoulders, I smiled down at her. She looked so genuinely sad that I didn't know what to do.

"Can't I come?" she asked.

"No," I said and gently squeezed her shoulders, "Dione, you'll find it boring, you don't like camping, there'll be lots of insects and animals and dirt and we both know you hate all those things."

There was no way in hell I was letting my eight-year-old sister come along with me on a camping trip with Callie. There was also no way in hell I was letting anybody ruin this trip for me. Ever since spring break started, I'd bored out of my mind, wandering aimlessly around the house in my pajamas and if I wasn't doing that I would be binging on Mad Men and America's Next Top Model. The door creaked open and I looked up to see Minnie walk in. She wasn't even paying attention to where she was going. She was fully engrossed on her cellphone, probably texting her latest boyfriend. Minnie was juggling was so many boys these days it was hard to keep up.

Minnie didn't look up from her phone as she said, "Can I have your room?"

I removed my hands from Dione's shoulders and stood up. "I'll be gone for like four days," I frowned at her, "not four years."

I knew Minnie would use my room to sneak her boyfriend in and I really didn't want to walk in on that again. I'd threatened to tell Mom because Minnie was fifteen and Mum had said no boyfriends until after high school. Of course, if I did that, she'd tell Mom I'd had two boyfriends in the last three years.

"So...I can have it?" Minnie said, popping the bubblegum in her mouth. That was another thing about my sister. She was always chewing bubblegum. She claimed it got rid of the unwanted calories in her cheeks. One of her friends who had recently gotten back from a holiday in Spain, said everyone in Europe was doing it. This was an obvious lie because I had googled it and all I found was an article about an old man who'd choked on gum and died.

"No," I snapped, "stay away from my room, Minnie."

I felt my cellphone buzz in the back pocket of my shorts. I pulled it out and read the text that had been sent. I smiled and slid it back into my pocket, "Callie's outside! I gotta go!"

I ignored Dione's pleas for me to stay and Minnie's questions about whether or not she could borrow some of my clothes for an upcoming party. I picked up my hefty rucksack and duffel bag and I darted out of my room. I said a quick goodbye to my mom who was in the kitchen shouting to somebody on the phone about her wedding dress, and eagerly left the house.

I paused just outside my door, my eyes landing on Callie's familiar blue Ford Fiesta parked in the street. Callie had passed her driving test pretty quickly. Dad wouldn't let me start learning until summer because he wanted me to focus on my studies. Minnie told me Dad was planning on giving me his old car, a beat up mustang that didn't even have an engine. She also said he wanted me to help him fix and repair it as some sort of father-daughter bonding session. Cars and mechanics or whatever just weren't my thing. It really made me wish they hadn't shipped my older brother off to military school. He should be the one helping Dad fix the mustang not me.

I skipped down the steps of my house and walked over to Callie. She was standing by the open trunk of the car, shifting some bags around. She looked up then and smiled when she saw me.

"Looking good, Peryn," she said.

I was all set for this camping trip. My dark hair had been pulled into a high ponytail, I was wearing a hoodie, denim shorts and a my favourite pair of doc martens. Although Callie was wearing a plain knee-length dress and high heeled boots, an outfit more suited for a house party than four days in the woods.

"I'm so excited!" I said, clapping my hands together in glee. "I bought so many marshmallows and my camera! We can take so many pictures and shove them in Savana Horowitz's face! Just because she spent a few weeks in South Africa she thinks she's Mother Teresa."

Callie's smile faltered as she looked nervously at me. "Uhm, Peryn, I meant to tell you," she said, "there's been a slight change of plan."

I stared at her, there was sudden an uneasy feeling in the pit of my stomach. "Slight change of plan?" My eyebrows rose, "we are still going right?"

"Oh yeah!" she beamed, "It's just that, well–"

"Callie!" A voice said.

My gaze skipped from an apprehensive looking Callie to the car and sitting in the front passenger seat was a dark haired boy greedily licking the ice cream that was melting onto his hands. It took me a few seconds to realize that this dark-haired boy was in fact Oliver Kaminski. He sat behind me in third period Spanish, he was the reason I was currently flunking that class. He smiled up at me, "Hey, Peryn."

I ignored his greeting and glanced at Callie, "What's he doing here?"

"Me and Jack are coming camping with you guys," Oliver answered.

My eyes widened, "Jack? "

And much to my horror I saw Callie's twin brother sitting in the back seat, who was lazily scrolling down his phone. As if sensing he was being watched, Jack's head instantly snapped up and his eyes met mine. The corners of his mouth tugged upwards into a small hesitant smile and my heart almost jumped into my throat. My eyes widened. What the hell was my ex-boyfriend doing here? I whipped around to face Callie.

"Callie," I said slowly. I think I already knew why they were here but I didn't want to believe it. "Callie, what's going on?"

"I know you wanted it to be just the two of us," she began, raising her hands up as a sign for me to calm down, "but when I told my mom about the camping trip she said no 'cause she didn't trust us by ourselves and the only way we could go is if we went with Jack and Jack decided to bring Oliver here! I had no choice, Per, I swear–"

"Hey guys," Oliver said, leaning his head out of the window so he could see us. His hand went up to his mouth as he cleared his throat, "uh, where's...uh, where's Ruby? I was told Ruby would be on this little trip."

Callie looked unimpressed, "is that the only reason you came? Because you thought Ruby would be here?"

Oliver had a crush on Ruby Blakewood for a little over two years now and he wasn't very subtle about it. Everyone knew he liked Ruby, everyone except Ruby herself. Watching Oliver Kaminski moon over her was not as entertaining as it used it be, these days it was just sad. Okay, it was like thirty percent still as entertaining.

"No! For your information, I happen to love nature and anyway, Jack invited me," he said a little defensively.

"I didn't," Jack spoke up, "you invited yourself."

Oliver glanced back at him, "can you not bust my balls here?" When Jack just rolled his eyes, Oliver turned back to us, "so, uh, is she here?"

Ruby was my cousin and had also been best friends with Callie and me since elementary school. Ruby's absence was the reason spring break felt so boring.

"No, she's not here Oliver," I told him, "she's gone to New York to stay with her mom for the week."

A month before spring break Ruby had even offered for me to come with her to New York to stay with her mom, who was my dad's older sister and to be honest my favourite out of all of Dad's siblings. I couldn't for the life of me remember why I had declined. How could I say no to two weeks in New York City?

Oliver swore and went back to licking his ice cream, this time unhappily. I sighed and looked back at Callie who was now wearing a sheepish expression.

"We still good to go?" she asked nervously. "I know it's not what you wanted but c'mon, we're already here, we might as well go."

I closed my eyes for a moment and took a deep breath. Okay, so there was a slight mishap, Two extra people had joined our camping trip, those two people just happened to be my ex-boyfriend and his goofy best friend. That was fine, I was totally cool with that. I had to be optimistic. I glanced back at my house and I contemplated giving up on this whole thing and just spending the rest of spring break watching marathons of The Bachelor. I looked at Callie, she was staring expectantly at me, her bright blue eyes wide and hopeful and she had this big sunny smile I always found hard to ignore. I sighed.

"Okay, whatever, let's get this stupid show on the road," I said, dumping my rucksack and duffle bag into the open trunk of the car.

Callie's smile grew brighter as she squeaked in excitement.

"Yes, Per!" she said as she slammed the trunk shut. She ran around the car, before opening the door to driver's seat she looked over at me and grinned. "You won't regret this!"

It was just for a few days, I told myself, what could possibly go wrong?

Chapter 4

I hadn't said anything to Jack since I hopped into the car. I mean, what was I supposed to say to him? What were you supposed to say to your ex-boyfriend? Jack and I had ended badly, so we never really spoke to each other, well any conversation was comprised of a simple yes or no and then we would try to get away from one another as quickly as possible. We'd said all we needed to say when we ended things two months ago.

I looked out of the car window, glumly watching the people and places that passed by. It was supposed to be just me and Callie on this camping trip. No one else. Obviously Callie didn't understand that. Actually, Ruby would be on this trip too but she was in New York. I contemplated whether or not it was too late to back out. I could make up some excuse about needing to help my mom with organizing the wedding. There was a crisis with the seating plan Mom had been freaking out over for two weeks now. It was a justifiable reason.

I frowned. That justifiable reason would have worked an hour ago when we were still in Vancouver. Callie was now happily driving the highway, so there was no turning back now.

"Aw come on guys!" Oliver said glancing back at us, "the sun is shining, Beyoncé is singing and it's a beautiful day for camping! Why are you so unhappy?"

Oliver couldn't stop laughing and jumping and singing like he was a little kid on Christmas day. It was hard to believe the boy was seventeen years old. Then again, Oliver Kaminski had always been immature and he was always making jokes or doing some stupid stunt. At school he had a reputation for being the class clown, the guy who could make anyone laugh in any situation.

The reason I was failing Spanish was because he was noisy and kept disrupting the lesson with some wise crack, that I admit even got me laughing sometimes. I think Oliver's hyperactive behaviour was due to all the energy drinks he had consumed. Callie was catching up with him, she was already on her fourth can and I dreaded to think just how hyperactive and antsy she would be in a few hours.

"Oliver, you need to stop with the energy drinks," Jack said, "You know you don't metabolize sugar well."

He snorted, "What are you talking about? I'm fine!"

"Dude, your left eye is twitching."

"Eyes do that!"

"No they don't," Jack said, "Just stop with the energy drinks."

Oliver rolled his eyes as he looked to the front again. He slumped back in his seat. "Sorry, Mom."

"Moron," Jack muttered.

Callie kept one hand on the wheel as she leaned forward and pressed a button on the radio, the Beyonce track that was playing instantly stopped and in its place came the upbeat sound of Super Bass by Nicki Minaj. It wasn't long before Callie and Oliver were rapping along to the song together. I stared at the two of them as their heads bobbed up and down in a ridiculous manner. Now they were taking turns in rapping the verses. Shaking my head, I returned to staring miserably out of the window. I started thinking about opening the car door and flinging myself out onto the highway.

I felt a gaze on me, light and niggling at the back of my neck. I turned and caught Jack's eyes for a split second before he instantly looked away, his eyes flicking down to the cellphone in his hands, there was a noticeable blush dusting his cheeks. My eyes narrowed. Had he been watching me? I batted the thought away and looked out of the window again.

My thoughts returning to means of escape from this camping trip and the excuses I could use. Did I even need an excuse? No. I could just open the car door and leap out right now. If Bruce Willis could do it and survive then so could I. For the second time, I felt the weight of Jack's gaze on me again. I frowned. What was his problem? I looked over at him. I expected him to look away but this time, he kept his attention on me.

"Can I help you?" I said, surprised at how irritated I sounded.

Jack scratched the back of his neck. The blush was still on cheeks, he always did look adorable when he blushed.

Dropping his hand, he cleared his throat and went back to playing his cellphone as he mumbled an apology to me. If my heart clenched a little at his shy apology then I didn't acknowledge it.

"How's the chess club?" I suddenly blurted out. I really wanted to fling myself out the car then. At the beginning of eleventh grade, Jack secured the role as president of the school's chess club and I remember how happy he'd been when he got it. He couldn't stop grinning and hugging me all day. He was so adorable.

Jack looked up at me, confusion on his face and bewildered that I was talking to him, "Uh...Good."

I nodded, "Good."

I didn't know what to say so I looked out of the window once more. It took me a few seconds to realize that we were slowing down. My eyes skipped to the front of the car where Callie was pulling over at the side of the highway.

"Callie," I said, "What are you doing?"

"Just being a Good Samaritan!" she chimed.

"What are you talking about?"

Oliver turned in his seat, the same bright smile as Callie's plastered on his face. I think they were both so deep into the energy drinks they were feeling euphoric. He lifted his hand and pointed to the outside of the window Jack was sitting next to, "Look, there he is!"

Jack and I looked where he was pointing. Callie had parked the car at the side of the highway as cars, trucks, coaches and various other means of transportation whizzed past us in a heated rush. I noticed a figure cautiously crossing the highway. I'm near-sighted so it was only until the figure was only a few feet away from the car that I could see him properly. My eyes widened when the person came into focus.

It was a man. A tall and overweight man with the scruffiest beard and grubbiest clothing I had ever seen. He was carrying several white Abercrombie and Fitch bags, he had man boobs and a pot bellying hanging out for all to see but the most disturbing thing about this man was the fact he wasn't a wearing a shirt, just a leather jacket that was way too small for him. His chest looked like the matted, clumpy hair you'd find in the bathroom sink. It made me feel sick.

Oh my God, I thought.

He was heading for our car. He was heading straight for our car.

"Callie," I hissed, "Callie! There's a weird half-naked homeless guy walking towards our car! Go! Go! Go!"

"Calm down, I invited him," she said.

I stared at her.

"You what!" Jack and I shouted in unison.

Callie jumped at our sudden shouts of indignation, she glanced back at us with a frown, "What's wrong with you guys?"

"W-what's wrong...w-with us?" I sputtered, "You're about to pick up a freaking hitchhiker! You've seen enough horror movies to know that nothing good ever happens when you pick up hitchhikers!"

She rolled her eyes, "You're overreacting! Remember what those women who came to school said? Be a Good Samaritan! When someone needs help, you offer it."

"Callie, those women were fucking crazy and you know it!" I said, "One of them punched Mrs. Roderick in the face."

"Well, Mrs. Roderick is an asshole," she said with a shrug, "you can't blame them. Hell, I've been planning on punching her since tenth grade."

Oliver nodded in agreement, "She's got a point there Peryn, Mrs. Roderick is an asshole."

"Doesn't mean they can punch a fifty-year-old woman," I almost hissed.

Callie shook her head, "This is good for our karma! You do something good and something good happens in return!"

"Callie, don't be stupid," Jack said in a calm tone, "you can't just go round picking up–"

The door on Jack's side was suddenly yanked open and the hitchhiker bent his head down to look at us. I squeaked. The sweat on his bare chest was glistening so much it almost blinded me. I blinked, staring at him with a slack jaw. He was even fatter and more horrifying close-up.

"How are you all doing?" the hitchhiker beamed. He grinned, revealing an array of blackened teeth.

"Come on in!" Callie said, "Jack, move up."

As the hitchhiker started climbing into the car, Jack immediately shuffled down towards me. Once the hitchhiker had sat himself down and shut the door, he grinned again. I moved again so I was pressed against the door and Jack did the same, trying his best to separate himself from the hitchhiker.

"Thanks for the help," the man said, "I've been standing there all day, so thank you!"

"No problem! Anything to help a fellow Canadian!" Callie smiled, "Where are you going?"

"You don't happen to be passing by a little town called Kamloops do you?" the man asked.

Callie nodded, "We actually are! Our campsite's near there!"

"Thanks so much!" The hitchhiker said, clapping his hands loudly and making Jack and I jump in our seats. "I'm Bosco by the way!"

"Pleasure to meet you Bosco," Oliver said and pointed to everyone as he introduced us, "That's Callie, Jack, Peryn and I'm Oliver."

The hitchhiker, Bosco, nodded and grinned at all of us, "Nice to meet you."

Jack and I just stared at him with open mouths. We looked at each other and I found an odd comfort when I saw he was just as freaked as me.

"And we're off!" Callie announced as she started driving down the highway.

If we were killed and chopped up by this Bosco guy, I was going to make sure Callie's afterlife was worse than any hell she could ever imagine. We'd been driving for a total of four hours with the hitchhiker riding in the back with Jack and I. Oliver and Callie had coaxed Bosco into singing along with them. It was traumatic. He was jiggling and waving his hands around and I'm pretty sure, one of Bosco's man boobs hit Jack in the face. I was finding it hard to concentrate or drown out the horrendous sound of singing because Jack was pressed up against my side. He smelt so familiar, so woodsy and clean and it was causing fluttering feelings I hadn't felt in a long time to return. I didn't like it one bit.

"Callie, we've been driving for four hours, we should have reached Kamloops by now," Jack said. She didn't respond, just continued bobbing her head to the music that was play-ing. Jack said her name again, "Callie!"

"Okay," she sighed, "Now, I-I don't want you guys to panic."

I eyed her suspiciously, "Why would we panic?"

"Because...we may or not be lost," she chuckled nervously.

"What?" I said.

"I missed the exit like three hours ago and I've been trying to find another ever since and, yeah, we're lost."

I gaped at her, "Are you kidding? So, for the past three hours you've been driving in the completely wrong direction and you didn't tell us?"

"I'm telling you now!" She said and she had the nerve to sound like we were the assholes.

I shook my head, "You have got to be–"

"Guys," Jack interrupted, "Look, I saw a sign for a gas station a few miles back, we'll just stop there and ask for directions, okay?"

Oliver nodded, "Yeah, I saw it too, it's near here."

He didn't seemed as distressed at the fact Callie had been driving in the wrong direction for three hours. I frowned when I realized he'd probably known this little fact from the beginning. I wouldn't be surprised if he was the one who'd suggested she didn't tell anyone.

"You guys stay here," I said, eagerly hopping out of the car, "I'll be back."

I shut the door behind me and began trudging towards the shop. As Jack had said, there was a gas station. It hadn't taken long to find it, only about ten minutes or so. Callie was parked by the main road, I glanced back at her, she grinned and threw me a thumbs up as some sort of encouragement. I rolled my eyes. It was empty and unnervingly quiet, the bell jingled as I entered the store. I approached the till where a scrawny man with a goatee was standing behind the counter.

I cleared my throat to get his attention. He looked up from the fishing magazine he was reading. I said, "Excuse me, uhm, do you know how to get to Kamloops?"

"The city?" he asked.

I nodded, "Yeah."

He laughed, "You're a long way away from there, sweet cheeks. You're long way away from anywhere, actually."

"Yeah, there's a camping site near Kamloops, my friends and I are a little lost, so do you know how to get there?"

"Just keep going straight and after two hours you should come to an intersection, take route two-ten and that should take you straight to Kamloops."

I nodded, "Okay, thanks!"

I threw him a grateful smile and walked out of the shop, repeating the directions in my head. I froze. Callie, Jack and Oliver were all standing outside with some of our bags by their feet. I frowned when I noticed the car wasn't where it had been parked. I looked around – in fact – the car was nowhere to be seen.

My eyebrows crumpled together as I looked at Callie in confusion, "Where's the car?"

Oliver chuckled, "You will not believe what happened."

I folded my arms across my chest, "Try me."

Jack started pacing up and down as he dragged a hand through his dark hair. He said, "We got robbed."

"What?" I said, not quite believing what I was hearing.

"Bosco took the car," he explained, "when you were in the store, he pulls out this revolver and tells out to get out of the car and as soon as we took our rucksacks out of the trunk, he drove off."

I waited for one of them to burst out laughing and tell me it was all a joke, that the car was just around the corner and that we could go home and forget this whole horrible ordeal. Of course none of that happened. They just stared back at me, looking as morose as ever.

"Oh my God," I breathed, "I told you not to pick up that bastard hitchhiker!"

"How was I supposed to know the guy was going to steal the car?" she snapped.

I threw my arms up in the air and let them flop to back down, "We're screwed! We are officially screwed!"

"Shit," Jack muttered as he continued pacing, "We'll need to call my mom, hopefully she can come to pick us up."

Callie's eyes widened, "No! Jack, she'll kill us!"

"And what do you suggest?" Jack said, swiveling round to face her, "We walk four hundred miles back home?"

"Four hundred miles isn't so bad," she grinned, "it'll be good exercise!"

"Nobody's walking home," I frowned at her, "We'll just have to call your mom, it'll be fine."

Callie ran towards me. She grabbed my hoodie and yanked me against her. Her blue eyes were wide with fright. She looked absolutely insane.

"Fine?" she hissed, "Per, my mom is going to disembowel us! Do you know how much that car cost? It is worth more than me and Jack's life combined! She will kill me!"

"Well, maybe, you should have thought of that before you picked up some random hitchhiker called Bosco," I said, prying her hands off of me and pushing her back. "What the hell kind of name is Bosco anyway?" I looked at Jack, "Damn it, call your mom."

"We tried using our cellphones, there's no signal," Jack said, "we'll have to use the store, maybe they have a phone."

"I'll come with you," I said.

I followed him as he turned and walked towards the store. He tried to push the door open but it wouldn't budge. I stepped next to him and I cupped my hands around my eyes and peered into the shop. I banged on the glass when I saw the owner sweeping up a few feet away. He looked up at me.

"Shop's closed," he said.

"What? No!" I shook my head fervently, "We need to use your phone! Our car got jacked and we need to call some-one."

The man frowned, "Sorry, shop's closed."

"Dude, it's only six o'clock," Jack said.

"Exactly," the man said, "Shop closes at six, and it's six o'clock now so the shop's closed."

"Please, we need to make a quick call, it will only take a few minutes," I pleaded.

"I'm sorry but the shop is closed, I have a shotgun and it would do you well not to piss me off," he said, "Come back tomorrow morning, the shop opens at six, I can help you then."

Despite our pleas and protests for him to help us, the man simply shook his head and went back to sweeping the floor. My forehead hit the door and I let out a long sigh.

"We'll have to come back tomorrow then," Jack concluded glumly.

I lifted my head off the glass window and glanced at him, "And where are we supposed to sleep Jack? On the floor?"

"We've got our camping gear," Jack said, "We can just camp out in the woods for tonight and come back tomorrow."

I groaned. I let my forehead hit the door again and again and again until I sighed again. This day could not get any better.

"Okay," I said, feeling defeated and angry, "looks like we're spending the night in the woods like a merry band of homeless people."

Chapter 5

My eyes sluggishly opened. I was lying on my back, looking up at the ceiling but the ceiling in my bedroom wasn't painted with pink hearts. Jesus, why the hell was everything so bright? There was too much sunlight, it cast the pink hearts on the ceiling everywhere, making everything look like some sort of dance club for Care Bears.

Confusion clouded my thoughts and questions popped up in quick instances. I slowly turned my head to the right, gasping sharply when I saw a familiar boy sleeping beside me. My head was resting on his outstretched arm and his other arm was lazily wrapped around my waist.

My drumming heart was in my throat as his eyelids fluttered open, big chocolate brown eyes that belonged to none other than Jack Marshall focused in on me. We just stared at each other, confused and not processing the situation for a few seconds before we both screamed. I wasn't sure if it was me or him who started the screaming but nonetheless, we scrambled away from one another faster than the speed of light. I sprang up just as he rolled away from me.

Jack raised his hands, palms facing me in a show of surrender. We stopped screaming and stared at each other.

I ignored the fact that he was only wearing his Superman boxers. I felt my heart flutter. He was such a geek, especially when it came to computers but even more so when it came to comics. There were his favorite; he wore them frequently when I would sleep over at his house but I had to admit, my favorite were his Batman boxers.

"Why the hell are you screaming?" he asked.

"What the hell are you doing in my room?" I countered.

I thanked God for my brown skin, because it meant that any blushing wasn't detectable. He was the only one who could ever conjure up that butterfly inducing feeling that people wrote novels about.

Jack frowned, "Does this look like your room, Peryn?"

I expected to see the striped walls of my bedroom surrounding us but my eyes widened I saw we weren't in my bedroom at all but in a tent. Tent? The same frown Jack was wearing, slowly formed on my lips. An infinite series of questions flew in my brain as I looked around. I suddenly gasped. My eyes widening as the events of the previous night came hurtling towards me faster than a speeding bullet.

The car really had been stolen by that bastard hitchhiker and we really did spend the night in the woods. We'd all had to sleeping in the same tent because Callie had lost the other two. They had rolled off down a hill and were now forever lost somewhere in the bushes. It had been so awkward, considering the tent wasn't even big enough. The four of us, had to squeeze ourselves in and Callie couldn't stop complaining about people's elbows and Oliver talked in his sleep. It was hell.

"It wasn't a dream," I said in disbelief, "It really happened, we really are stranded four hundred miles from home."

"Peryn," he said my name so softly, the way he used to do when he was worried about me, it made my heart jump in my chest.

"I need some air," I said. I turned and unzipping the flap, I crawled out of tent. I stood up as soon I was out. Stretching my arms, I took in the never-ending stream of trees, the sound of birds chirping and bees humming, the smell of wood and smoke dancing in the morning air. I lifted my face, letting the light and shadow dance across my dark skin. In different circumstances, I would have been enjoying the nature around me, reveling in the peace and -

"Peryn!"

I jumped. I swiveled round, facing the direction the voice had come from and not far ahead, Oliver was sitting on one of the logs by the campfire. Last night, it had taken almost two hours to light the fire all because he wouldn't let anybody else try and by the end of it, Jack had to wrestle the wood off of him.

"You okay Oliver?" I asked as I approached him.

He nodded, "Didn't sleep too well, way too cramped in there." He rubbed his eyes, "if only Callie hadn't lost the other tent."

I sat on the log beside him and sighed, "Yeah, me too."

Oliver leaned back, he picked up a bag from behind him and placed it on his lap. He pulled the zip open and passed me a packet of potato chips and took out one of himself. He then pulled out two cans of coke.

"When did you buy this?" I said.

"Took a detour to the store before we went to pick you up," he said.

Oliver and I sat in silence, eating the potato chips and drinking the coke as we listened to the lulling sound of nature.

"Hey, how cool is this?" Oliver asked as he waved a pocket knife in my face, "it's gold plated dude, I got it from that pawn shop across from Lemon & Lime."

"That pawn shop is really shady Oliver," I said, "Ammara Ali told me they have an illegal gambling room in the back."

He grinned, "I know, that's why I like it."

"Where's Callie?" Jack asked as he clambered out of the tent.

"She said she needed to pee," Oliver answered through a mouthful of potato chips.

I was finding it hard to tear my eyes away from Jack. I had always thought he looked the best in the mornings. All messy hair and his deep voice thick with sleep. He was fully dressed now in jeans, converses and a light grey sweater. Jack's eyes met mine and I instantly looked away, feeling a little embarrassed to be caught staring.

"Right," I said, "I'm getting changed."

There was no shower, but I wasn't staying in these sweaty clothes from yesterday. I entered the tent. I rummaged through my rucksack and I dressed myself in some cute floral print shorts I'd gotten from Forever 21 and a white crop top. It was a pretty hot day, so I could just dress lightly.

I quickly brushed my hair back and pulled it into a high ponytail. Once I finished tying the shoelaces of my converses, I existed the tent. Jack and Oliver were sat on the logs, talking to one another. I walked over and took out a packet of wine gums from the duffel bag. I glanced at Jack, my breathing hitching at the sight of the glasses he was wearing.

"You're wearing your glasses again?" I questioned.

He look at me, the sunlight caught in eyes, bringing out hues of greens and gold amongst the dark brown.

"Yeah, not a fan of the contact lenses, why?" He grinned a little shyly, "Do I look bad?"

I was in no way admitting that he looked handsome in those glasses, that he always looked handsome in those glasses. I looked away, trying to sound and act as nonchalant as possible as I replied with a shrug, "Meh."

Just then we heard the sound of footsteps. For a moment I was worried that it might be a wolf but I was thankful to find that it was Callie who appeared from the path lined with shrubbery and trees. She trudged towards us with that trademark grin plastered onto her face. I stood up, grimacing a little. She was holding something in her arms, no more like she was cuddling something. Something brown and furry. Jack and Oliver stood up, noticing the furry thing in her arms as well.

"What is that?" Oliver pointed to the ball of fur.

Callie smiled down at it, "It's a bear."

"I'm sorry?" Jack said, blinking rapidly.

"It's a bear," she repeated, "Well, a bear cub, it's so cute! I was looking for a distant spot to pee and I just saw it wandering around looking so lost and scared, so I thought I would take it."

"Take it?" I said, "You can't just take a wild bear."

"Why not? His mother's obviously abandoned him and he has a name," she said, looking unreasonably smug, "Winston the Bear."

"Winston," Oliver mused, "It a good name and she's right, Winston is really cute, just look-"

Oliver's sentence was cut short by the glares Jack and I simultaneously threw him. The bear made a soft mewling noise as it wriggled in Callie's arms.

"Aw, are you hungry Winston?" She cooed.

"What," I shrugged, "are you just going to adopt it? Do you plan to keep it forever?"

Jack stared at her, "Callie, what are you even -"

"AH ZABENYA!" she shouted as she raised it up in the air like it was Simba from the Lion King. "AH ZABENYA! BA-BA BEECHI BA-BA YA!"

"Oh my God," I whispered, my fingers going to nip the bridge of my nose as Callie continued to sing the Circle of Life.

She didn't even know the words, let alone what she was saying. It was ridiculous.

"I, Callisto Eve Marshall!" She declared in the most obnoxious voice she could muster, "Daughter of Luna and Rosalie Marshall! Twin sister of Jack Edward Marshall, hereby announce Winston the Bear to be my child! This is legally binding!"

"Damn it Callie, put that bear down," Jack said. Callie glared at him but she lowered the bear into her arms anyway.

"This is crazy," I said, "You're not keeping that bear, you need to put it back where you found it."

"Uh, guys," Oliver said.

"You know the rules; finders, keepers," Callie replied as she held the bear closely again.

"Guys."

"It's not some toy, it's a wild animal, "Jack said, "you can't just take an animal like this out of its natural habitat! It's dangerous!"

"Guys."

Callie frowned, "You don't understand, me and Winston have made a bond, he thinks of me as his mother now."

"Guys."

"Are you insane?" I hissed, "Nobody is going to let you keep this wild animal, what-"

"Guys!" Oliver suddenly snapped.

We all looked at him. I raised my eyebrows, "What?"

Oliver's jaw was slack, and he looked petrified as he stared at something behind us. He sputtered, "Look!"

We turned on our heels, following the horrified direction of his grey eyes. Jack's eyes widened, I gasped and Callie squeaked at the gigantic bear that stood several feet away. When I said this bear was gigantic, I meant it, this thing was colossal and there was evil in its soulless eyes. The four of us just standing there, staring in shock at the bear, who, in return, was staring back at us. Its lips peeled back, snarling venomously as it eyed us greedily. The earth shattering roar that escaped its mouth was enough to spring us into action.

"Run!" Jack shouted, "Run!"

I didn't need to be told twice. We turned in the opposite direction and began running away from the bear. The trees flashed by me, my heart beating fast in my chest as I pumped my legs forward.

Callie was clutching the bear cub to her chest as she screamed, "Oh my God, it's chasing us!"

Jack was the fasted out of all us, he was in front in no time and so we all just followed. Running behind him, cursing and shouting as we were chased by a ravenous angry bear.

"Callie!" Jack shouted, "It wants the bear cub! It wants Winston! It must be the mother!"

"But I'm the mother! He needs me!" Callie cried.

"No, you're not! What you need to do is give Winston back to his real mother!"

I could hear the thundering steps of the bear as it continued to chase us. Callie was running just a few steps behind me. I glanced back at her, my eyes wide as I shouted, "This is insane! Just give the bear its baby!"

She pouted, holding the bear closer, "But - what if it eats Winston!"

"It's going to rip us apart and eat us if you don't!" Oliver yelled, "Do you want to us to die? Give the fucking bear its baby!"

I jumped over a tree stump, my heart jumping to my throat when I nearly tripped on a stray branch. I stumbled and I thought I was going to crash on the floor face first but I luckily regained my footing and kept on running. The bear roared and we all screamed. Oh my God. I was going to be mauled to death by a bear because my best friend was a complete moron.

"Callisto!" I shouted, "we will feed you to the damn bear if it comes down to it!"

"Oh fine!" She snapped. She stopped for a split second to kiss the top of cub's head and place it down on the floor before she turned and continued running. "There! Have your baby!"

I glanced behind me. The bear came to a slow halt when it reached the cub. We all stopped running, standing a good distance away to watch the bear and its cub. Everybody was panting hard, trying to catch their breath. Jack was leaning against a tree, Oliver and Callie were bent over with hands on their knees and I had my hands on my hips, our breathing ragged and uneven.

"Look," Callie panted, "it's leaving."

She was right, the bear and the cub were turning round, slowly heading back to whatever pit they came from. I huffed out a breath of relief, "Oh thank God, I actually thought I was going to die."

"Goodbye Winston," Callie croaked, sounding a little heart-broken.

"That's right!" Oliver shouted out of nowhere, "Leave you little bitch! Nobody wants you here!"

"Oliver!" Jack hissed.

"No! That little bitch needs to learn not to mess around with-"

The bear had suddenly turned around and began speeding towards us, snarling and gnashing its spectacularly sharp teeth. Callie screamed. The four of us instantly started running. My surroundings blurred, my heart banging deafeningly loud in my chest and my breathing ragged as we tore through the woods, from the terrifying roar and the thunderous footsteps the bear wasn't far behind us.

"Oliver, you asshole!" Jack cried, "Why the hell did you say that?"

"I didn't think it would be bothered! You would think bears have bigger problems than being called little bitches!" He responded.

"If you just kept your stupid mouth shut!" I snapped.

"It's not my fault!" he said, "since when can bears understand English?"

"If we die, I'm going to make sure you burn in hell Kaminski!" Callie shouted.

We ran and ran, not daring to stop for even a second in fear of the bear devouring our bodies. I don't how or when, but after, what felt like, an eternity, we somehow managed to lose the bear.

"I-I t-think...I think...w-we lost...it..." I said in between large intakes of air.

Oliver dropped to his knees and lay on the grassy ground. Jack slid down the trunk of a tree and slumped onto the floor. Callie kicked Oliver's leg.

"Ow!" He cried, "What the hell?!"

"That's for calling Patricia a little bitch."

"Who the fuck is Patricia?"

"Winston's mother, I named her Patricia," she said.

"I'm sorry," Oliver grunted, "but I name it how I see it and that bear is a little bitch!"

I frowned, spinning as I looked around the endless trees that surrounded us, "Wait a second, do...do you guys know where we are?"

Callie's eyes widened, "Oh my God, no, I can't...I don't know where we are."

"I know where we are!" Oliver beamed as he pushed himself up, "Nowhere, Middle of!"

"Oh, be serious!" Callie grunted roughly punched his shoulder. He cried in pain, rubbing the spot where she had hit him as he glared at her and muttered some curses under his breath.

"Nobody was paying attention to where we were going?" I asked.

"Well forgive us Peryn but we were kind of busy running for our lives from a crazy bear," Oliver said.

"Yep," Jack said. He raked a hand through his dark hair, tugging at it the way he did when he was frustrated, "We're lost."

I didn't know whether to laugh, cry, or die.

Death seemed to be the quickest way out of this predicament.

Chapter 6

"I'm tired," Callie whined.

I sighed, "yeah, we heard you first the fifty times Callie, you don't have to keep saying it."

"But," Callie said and even though I was walking several steps in front of her, I knew she was pouting, "I'm–"

"Don't finish that sentence Callie," I said.

I glanced back at her and saw that she was indeed pouting just like I'd suspected.

"Well what do you want us to do Callie?" I said, "we're all tired, we've been walking for God knows how long and–"

"One hour and twenty-two minutes," Oliver said.

I looked at him, "what?"

He lifted his arm and I saw a blue watch strapped to his wrist. "We've been walking for one hour and twenty-two minutes," he said, "I've been keeping track."

I peered at it, "is that a Power Rangers watch?"

Oliver instantly dropped his hand and shoved it into the pockets of his cargo pants. He shook his head, "no....maybe...maybe not what's it to ya?"

I just stared at him for a few seconds. "Right..." I said slowly and looked back at Callie, "just stop complaining, this is already hard enough without you moaning every five minutes about your feet."

As Oliver had stated, we'd been walking for a while and none of us knew where we were. We'd started walking in any direction – because they all looked the same to be honest – in hope we'd find our campsite. I was scared we would run into that bear again but I knew Callie was kind of hoping we would because she kept saying how much she missed holding the bear cub in her arms.

Looking back, I realize blindly going in any direction without much planning was a bad idea but we were all a little traumatized from the run in with a huge bear and hungry since we hadn't had anything good to eat since we'd left Vancouver. So, I think we could be forgiven for acting so thoughtlessly.

Actually, it was Oliver who'd decided which direction we should walk and we had all been stupid enough to follow him. It had escaped my mind that Oliver Kaminski never knew what he was doing. Oliver Kaminski never planned. He was a huge moron like that.

"Okay, I'll stop complaining if one of you gives me a piggy back," she said with a hopeful smile.

I didn't even respond to her. I turned and looked ahead at the endless trees that lay before and around us. There were too many and I was getting sick of looking at them. Nearly two hours of walking and everything looked the same, it felt like we were going round in circles.

"No one's giving you a piggy back Cal," Jack said. It was the first thing he'd said in a while. For the most part he'd been walking in silence with his hands in his pockets, staring resolutely ahead. He was the furthest ahead out of all us, at some point we had all started following him.

Although I don't know why, Jack was just as clueless as the rest of us. I'd thought about saying something to him, but every time I was a few steps away I panicked and fell back into my original place next to Oliver. I wouldn't know what to say anyway. Things were already hard enough, I didn't need to add awkwardness into the mix.

Oliver looked like he was giving Callie's offer some serious thought. He looked at her, "If I give you a piggy back will you stop complaining?"

She nodded, "totally."

This should be interesting, I thought as I watched Oliver pause and Callie walk over to him. Oliver was shorter than Callie. He stood at five foot seven, whilst Callie was a little over five foot ten. Oliver grunted when she gracelessly hopped onto his back.

He stumbled and nearly fell. I'm guessing he realized Callie was heavier than she looked. After a few seconds, Oliver seemed to adjust to her weight and I was surprised at how easily he was able to carry her. For a guy who skipped out on gym almost every week with some lame excuse about his knees, he was in way better shape than I thought.

Callie laughed, "Wow, Oliver you're pretty strong."

I couldn't tell if she was being sincere or if she was just flirting to make sure he kept carrying her. Knowing Callie it was probably both.

"Thanks," he smirked, "I work out."

"No you don't," Jack said.

Oliver threw him a half-hearted glare, "I do!"

Jack opened his mouth to argue but Callie beat him to it, "Jude works out y'know. He goes to the gym like every week."

I think we all grimaced at the mention of Jude Sinclair. Oliver said, "okay, another part of the deal is you're not allowed to talk about him."

Callie looked like she was going to protest but she gave up at the last second and nodded, "okay, your back your rules right?"

So, we continued walking. Aimlessly wandering through woods like a band of homeless ghosts. Oliver's pace had slowed since he'd allowed Callie to hop onto his back, so he was a few steps behind me. We walked for another half-hour before Oliver finally gave up and told Callie he couldn't carry her anymore. Jack and I were just as tired. I felt like my feet were going to fall off if I didn't stop.

"Okay," I said, stumbling over to rest by one of the trees, I slid down onto the grassy floor, "let's a take break because I can't physically walk anymore."

Callie left Oliver and came over to sit next to me. She dropped her head on my lap and let out the longest yawn. "I'm so tired," she whispered, "and thirsty and hungry and–"

"What did we say about complaining Callie," I said. She grumbled something that sounded vaguely apologetic. I rested my hand on her head and started to card my fingers through her rich blonde hair. It was automatic, something I always did whenever Callie placed her head on my lap or my shoulders.

Oliver dropped to the floor where he was standing. He rolled onto his back and let out the loudest sigh as he looked up at the trees. You couldn't see much of the sky since it was hindered by branches and leaves but from the small glimpses here and there, it seemed to be a bright cloudless blue, which was good news because the last thing we needed was rain. Jack slumped down next to Oliver. He rested his elbows on his knees and glanced over at me. Our eyes met and he instantly looked away. His attention flitted to the grass he'd started to pull from the ground.

"I'm gonna die," Oliver whined, "I'm actually going to die here."

"No whining," I reminded him. "No one is allowed to whine."

The four of us stayed like that for a while. I don't know for how long but it was nice. I mean, ignoring the fact we were completely lost in the forest and had been for the past two hours, it was peaceful. I was sitting on the floor with my back against the tree trunk and Callie lightly snoozing on my lap with my fingers in her hair. Jack and Oliver were both lying on the floor, quietly talking to another about Grand Theft Auto V. I lifted my head and closed my eyes. The sunlight dappling through the branches of the tree landed on my face, warming my dark skin.

"We're going to try and get a signal on our phones," Jack said. I opened my eyes to find Jack and Oliver had stood up. They were both holding their cellphones in their hands. "There's a hill just over there, if we hold our phones in the right positions we should able to get some signal."

I nudged Callie awake. She groaned and lifted her head off my lap. She rubbed her eyes. "Wha?"

"These two are going to try and get signal on their phones," I told her and I looked back at them, "you going to call for help?"

Jack nodded, "we should able to." He turned and started walking off, "c'mon Oliver."

"If we're not back in five minutes it's safe to assume we've been killed."

Jack glared at him, "don't say that."

Oliver shrugged, "What? Am I not allowed to speak the truth now?"

They disappeared behind a thick line of bushes, I could still hear their arguing voices but a few seconds later that was gone too. I was left in silence with a sleepy Callie Marshall. She yawned and sat up fully, stretching her arms and almost hitting me in the face with her elbow.

"Holy shit," she blinked rapidly, "how long have I been asleep?"

"I don't know, I lost track of time," I said, "the only person with a watch is Oliver."

Callie shifted closer to me so she could rest her back on the tree as well. We were quiet again. There was only the sound of birds singing in the distance and sensation of the spring wind swimming by.

"You know," Callie said, rubbing her eyes once more, "you're doing a great job of pretending like Jack doesn't exist. It's actually pretty funny, you're so awkward around him."

I looked at her. She was glancing down at her nails like they were the most fascinating things in the world. "Am I awkward?" I asked her with wide eyes, "Shit, I was going for you know, nonchalant but also not douchey."

Callie laughed, "Seriously? Well you're failing terribly."

My eyes narrowed, "well I wouldn't even be having this problem if you hadn't invited him."

"What was I supposed to do Per?" she asked, "you know how scary my mom is."

Callie had two moms but I knew which one was she was talking about. Rosalie Marshall was a hard-hearted woman, tough to please with a sense of humour that was almost non-existent. I guess you'd have to be if you were head of the Vancouver Police Department. Callie's second mom, Luna Marshall, was a little softer and more understanding than her wife since she did work as a pediatrician but she could be just as stubborn when it came down to it.

"Mom wouldn't let me go," Callie said, "but then Ma said I could if I had some kind of adult supervision."

"But I'm older than you."

"I told Ma, but she was like you can go if you take Jack with you, Jack is old enough," she said, "me and Jack are twins, he is literally like two minutes older than me but my moms will never, ever let me forget that."

I put my head in my hands, "this trip was a terrible idea! This is what happens in horror movies! A group of teens go on a trip and then they're picked off one by one by a chainsaw wielding maniac with a fetish for human skin."

"Jesus, Peryn." Callie sounded appalled.

I felt like crying, "but it's true!"

Callie patted my head rather patronizingly, "there, there."

Callie had always been terrible when it came consoling people, she was better at cheering them up. Frowning, I pushed her hand off my head and looked up. It was then that I saw the familiar figures of Jack and Oliver come into view. It took an embarrassingly long time for me to push myself up to a standing position.

"Per," Callie said, motioning for me to help her. I took her hand and with a grunt I pulled her up. "Oh God, my knees are killing me.

"Any luck?" I asked them but from their sullen expressions I guessed not.

Oliver shook his head, "we could barely get any signal."

"But I do know we're somewhere in Wells Gray Provincial Park," Jack said, "I'd say about four hundred miles from Van-couver."

"What? We're so far away!" Callie wailed.

"Oh Vancouver!" Oliver cried dramatically as he raised his fists in the air, "Sweet Vancouver! We will come back to you!"

They started shouting Vancouver in unison like howling monkeys. I ignored Oliver and Callie's hysterics and turned to Jack. "So, what do we do?" I asked him.

Jack glanced at me, surprised I was talking to him. He cleared his throat and said, "uh, well, the nearest town is Linbeach, which is thirty-one miles west of here. That's our best bet."

"And how long will that take?" I said.

"Twelve hours give or take," he said, "there's no point in looking for our campsite, we won't find it, we need to head to Linbeach."

I hated the fact he was right. I really didn't want to walk for thirty miles. I don't know if my feet could take it.

I nodded, "okay."

I looked at Callie and Oliver who were whimpering and pouting because we were so far home. "Well," I said, "let's start walking guys."

"I'd like to build the world a home and furnish it with love!" My voice echoed in the woods, "Grow apple trees and honey bees and snow white turtle doves!"

I was singing. Singing terribly off key but at this point I just didn't care.

"Take it Callie!" I said, pointing to her.

"I'd like to teach the world to sing in perfect harmony!" Callie grinned, "I'd like to hold it in my arms and keep it company!"

I laughed and started to clap my hands in beat to the song. I pointed to Oliver, "Take it Kaminski!"

Oliver opened his mouth, "I'd like to see the world for once all standing hand in hand! And hear them echo through the hills for peace throughout the land!"

I never realized until now but Oliver was an amazing singer. Some time in ninth grade, a little after Jude Sinclair had tackled him to the ground for insulting his hair, Oliver had formed an indie-rock type band with three of his friends, two of whom were from the neighbouring schools. A band unfortunately named Fat Monkey Heart.

"All together now!" I said.

"That's the song I hear!" Callie, Oliver and I sang in unison as we clapped, "Let the world sing toda-a-a-a-a-y!"

"It's official," Jack said, ducking under a low branch, "you've lost your minds."

We'd been walking for almost an hour and I'd noticed the group morale was dangerously low, even Callie was moping, which was rare because Callie was the most optimistic person I knew. If Callie lost that energy everyone fed off we would truly be lost. So, I decided to take matters into my own hands and I started singing. Music was a great soother and I knew Callie was the master at karaoke and Oliver was the lead singer of Fat Monkey Heart.

It didn't take long until they were singing along with me and smiling. Jack just flat out refused to join in. He never wanted to do anything fun, always so serious, always sticking by rules and never taking any risks. When we were together I always used to tell him, all work and no play makes Jack a very dull boy. I thought it was my best joke, he didn't.

I continued clapping, if only to annoy him, "I'd like to teach the world to sing in perfect harmony!"

"I'd like to build the world a home and furnish it with love!" Oliver sang, his deep voice ringing out in the empty woods.

Jack froze, his head snapping up, "what was that?"

Callie lifted her arms in the air, "Grow apple trees and honey bees and –"

Jack slapped a hand over Callie's mouth, "shush!"

Her arms fell to the side as she gave a muffled and indignant reply. Jack removed his hand from her mouth. She glared at him, "what the hell is your problem Jack?"

He either ignored her or he wasn't listening. Jack stood still as his dark brown eyes flickered all over the place. He lifted a finger to his lips, "can you hear that?"

"Hear what?" Oliver asked with furrowed eyebrows.

"I don't know, but I heard something over there," he said and nudged his thumb to the thick shrubbery.

We were all silent, waiting to hear anything out of the ordinary but when a few seconds passed, Oliver shook his head. "Nah," he said, "you must have imagin–"

The shrubbery shook and it shook again. There was something in the shrubbery. A low growling noise emanated and my eyes widened. I took a step back, automatically moving towards to Jack so that our shoulders were pressed together. I felt his warm skin on mine, it was comforting.

"Shit," Callie whispered. The shrubbery shook again and the growling became louder.

"Nobody move," Jack said, "I'm sure it'll go away if we –"

In a blur, something grey and furry with sharp teeth and a huge snapping mouth leaped out from the bush and we all screamed.

Chapter 7

Jack grabbed a hold of my hand and turning on his heel he ran, pulling me along with him. Oliver was already zooming past us. How the hell was he was so fast? He never did anything exercise related and yet he was the fastest in the group.

"Holy shit!" I shouted, "is that a fucking wolf!"

"No!" Oliver said and quickly glanced behind him, "it's about four fucking wolves!"

This only made Callie screamed louder. We zipped through the trees, everything became a blur and my heart drummed painfully hard in my chest. Fear propelled me to move faster. I was not going to die today but I really didn't think we could outrun them.

"This way!" Jack shouted as he took a dramatic turn to the right. "I've got an idea!"

I heard the sound of the rushing water before I saw it. There was a huge river ahead of us and I suddenly understood his idea.

I shook my head, "no!"

"Are you crazy? No fucking way!" Callie panted, she glanced at him and then at the speeding wolves behind us, "yes fucking way!"

"Wait, what?" Oliver said, "what's the plan now?"

"We're going to jump into the river!" I told him.

Oliver's hazel eyes widened, "No fucking way!"

"Listen!" Jack shouted over our panicked conversation, "we can't outrun the wolves, so unless you want to get eaten, follow me!"

He headed towards the river and since he was holding onto my hand so tightly, I followed him. We came to the edge of the rushing river, Oliver zipped past us and jumped straight into the water without a moment's hesitation. Callie leaped in after him with a terrified scream, but I had come to a halt. My eyes were wide and it felt like my heart was going to burst out of my chest from how hard it was beating.

Jack looked at me. "Peryn," he said, "do you trust me?"

"What? I - "

"Do you trust me?" he repeated. I could barely hear anything over the sound of my heartbeat.

I stared at him, "yes but Jack -"

"Get in the fucking river you idiots!" Callie screamed. Oliver and Callie had latched onto a large chunk of wood that had been floating on the water. "They're right behind you!"

Movement snapped back into my limbs. If it was possible I held onto Jack's hand tighter and ran forward, we jumped into the river together just as the pack came barking and gnashing near our feet. All the air was knocked out of my lungs, the freezing water swallowed our bodies. I started panicking when I noticed Jack's hand had left mine. I couldn't scream or the water would flood into my mouth. I kicked my legs as hard as I could and swam up to the surface. I was coughing and sputtering as my head whipped back and forth.

"Peryn!" Oliver shouted.

I looked to the left. I almost sank back down from sheer relief when I saw Jack, Oliver and Callie all clinging to the large chunk of wood. Callie and Jack reached over and grabbing both my wrists, they hauled me over. I floated next to Jack and tightly held onto the wood. Callie and Oliver were on one side of the wood and Jack and I were on the other. The river was quickly carrying us downstream. We were all soaking wet and breathing hard. Jesus. The water so cold, I was starting to shiver. The wolves had stopped chasing after us, they were standing on the edge of the river, barking and looking angrier than before.

Oliver laughed and pointed to the wolves, "yeah, fuck you! Fuck you dumb mongrels! This is what you get don't mess with humans! We're the dominant life form on this damn planet for a reason you little bitches!"

Callie frowned, "Oliver can you stop calling crazy blood-thirsty animals that are trying to kill us little bitches?"

"Why?" he said, and shouted loud enough for his voice to echo, "they are little bitches! Every one of them!" he laughed again, "we're smarter than you will ever be! We won you dumb bitches!"

"Uh, I don't think it's time to celebrate just yet Oliver," Jack said, his wide eyes were glued ahead.

We all turned to see what he was looking at, Callie gasped, Oliver's jaw dropped and my eyes nearly bulged out of their sockets.

"Oh my God," I whispered.

There was a waterfall several feet away and the river was carrying us straight to it.

"Oh, great idea Jack!" Oliver snapped.

"I didn't know there was a waterfall here!" Jack barked at him, "did you want to get eaten by those wolves?"

"Does it matter now? We're going to die!"

Callie was panicking, "there has to be a way we can get out!"

"How the hell are we supposed to get out Callie?" I said, "We are floating on a junk piece of wood in river that's moving like two hundred kilometres per hour! There is no way we can get off!"

Callie sputtered, she held onto the log with one hand and used the other to push her soaked blonde hair out of her eyes, "what the hell are you talking about Peryn! This river is not moving at two hundred kilometres per hour!"

"Oliver we're not going to die!" Jack shouted.

He snorted, "last time I checked you weren't psychic Jack!"

"Neither are you!"

"If I wanted to, I could totally somersault off this log and jump onto dry land!" Callie said.

If I wasn't so terrified for my life, I would have laughed in her face. "Bullshit!"

"It's not bullshit!"

"Oh yeah?" I said, "Then do it Callie! Go on, somersault off this log and jump onto dry land!"

She huffed, "I don't have to prove anything to you Peryn!"

I pointed a finger at her, "that's because you can't do it!"

We were all so busy arguing with each other we failed to notice that we were getting closer and closer to the waterfall. I was shouting at Callie and Callie was shouting at me. Jack was shouting at Oliver and Oliver was shouting at Jack. It was a really messy situation that benefited no one but the four of us were so deeply engrossed in our nonsensical arguments that we seemed to forget the real danger we faced.

It was only at the last second, when the sound of the rushing water became almost deafening and drowned out our angry voices that we realized we had reached the waterfall. We were pushed us off the edge and we all fell. I opened my mouth to scream but water swallowed any sounds I could make. There was the distinct feeling gravity disappearing and the feeling of crashing through a mix of spilling water and cold air. I felt my organs spin as I fell. I thought I was going to die. I expected to land on cold hard ground and my head to split open, instead I plummeted into icy waters.

For several seconds I scrambled to get my bearings, everything was dark and blue and I didn't know which way was up. I saw bars of light come through so I followed that. I soon broke through the surface of the water, gasping and coughing so hard I thought my lungs would collapse. I whipped my head back and forth, trying to make sense of my surroundings and I saw, I'd landed in a large lake. The waterfall was behind me, spewing crashing waves of water that disorientated me.

"Peryn!"

I instantly turned in the direction the voice had come from. Callie was standing on the edge of the lake, looking as soaked and exhausted as I felt. I somehow managed to find the energy in me to kick my legs and swim over to her.

I sputtered when I reached land, crawling onto the stony, pebbled ground. I collapsed and rolled onto my back so that I was looking up at the sky. It was clear and bright and bluer than I had ever seen it. Callie stumbled over, she fell and landed on top of me. I grunted as she wrapped her arms around me and hugged me tightly.

"Peryn!" she cried, "oh thank God you're okay! I was scared you'd...y'know."

I patted her back. "I'm fine," I said. God, my voice was so hoarse, "are you okay?"

She nodded, her cheek was pressed up against mine. "Yeah, I'm fine."

"Okay," I chuckled, "okay, space, you're gonna kill me."

Callie's hugs were always so tight but warmer and better than anyone else's. She let go of me and I pushed myself up so I was kneeling on the ground. I looked around, expecting to see Oliver and Jack but I saw no signs of them.

"Callie," I said, "where's-"

"Hey!"

We looked up and my heartbeat rose. It was Oliver's voice but for some reason it sounded faraway. Callie broke into a grin as she pointed to the other side of the lake, where Oliver must have washed up because he was sitting on a boulder as he waved his arms up and down.

"Oliver!" Callie leapt up and waved her arms up and down as well. She cupped her hands around her mouth and shouted, "Are you okay?!"

"Yeah!" he said, "I mean, I just fell off a waterfall and drowned and I think I've broken a few ribs but apart from that I'm fine!"

I frowned. Where the hell was Jack? My eyes kept scanning where Oliver had washed up but I couldn't spot Jack.

"Callie," I said, I could feel the panic rising in my chest, "Callie, where's Jack?"

She froze. Her wide grin faltering for a second as her bright blue eyes snapped over to me, "I-I don't know." She looked back to Oliver, "Hey is my brother with you?"

There was a pause, which I didn't take as a good sign, before Oliver answered, "I thought he was with you."

"Oh my God," I whispered as it suddenly dawned me, on all of us that Jack probably hadn't made it out of the lake. I felt like I was going to throw up. I didn't even stop to think as I stood up and ran back to the lake. I dived into the water. It was colder than before and the impact of hitting the water so hard, knocked the wind out of my lungs. I didn't stop to collect myself, I just kicked and swam deeper into the lake. It was dark and murky under the water. My heart rate was rising as I tried to locate Jack. I glanced back and forth but I saw no sign of him.

I was just about to go up to the surface for some air when I spotted his familiar figure. He had passed out and was slowly sinking to the bed of the lake. I swam over to him as quickly as I could, and when I reached him, I slipped my arm around his waist and placing his own arm on my shoulders, I swam up. I could feel my lungs burning, I needed air now or I would find myself drowning too. I broke the surface and let out the loudest gasp as I sucked in as much as air I could. Jack's head lolled onto my shoulder.

I coughed and pushed my soaked hair out of my eyes. I think Callie and Oliver were shouting my name but I was too busy trying to catch my breath and keep Jack and I afloat. Once I brought some air back into my lungs, I held onto Jack tighter and swam over to the lake's shore. Callie and Oliver were there, they ran forward and helped me out. I looked at Jack who he was lying on the ground, eyes closed and completely motionless.

"Shit, fuck, fuck," Oliver said, lowering his head down to Jack's face, "he isn't breathing."

I quickly pushed him away and knelt down beside him. I was suddenly and unquestionably thankful for all the first aid lessons Dad had drilled into me when I was a kid. I kept Jacks chin tilted up with one hand as I used the other to pinch his nose shut. I inhaled and sealed my mouth over his. I breathed in and I breathed in again. I quickly pulled away and placed my hands flat on his chest as I started pushing down, hard and fast.

I counted to thirty and breathed into his mouth again, then moved back to pumping his chest. I kept doing this, praying he would be all right as Oliver and Callie stared in horror. Fear settled at the pit of my stomach when I started thinking this wasn't working, that Jack was already gone and there was nothing I could do.

Then, Jack's whole body jolted and he started to splutter. I looked at him with wide eyes as he coughed out water. He gasped at the same time Callie squealed happily. Jack pushed himself up onto his elbows and let out a string of coughs. He looked a little bleary eyed and dazed. His gaze flitted all over the place, and I could tell he was trying to make sense of what just happened.

His eyes landed on me, dark brown irises meeting mine and I felt waves upon waves of relief crash over me. I don't know what happened but something in me just snapped.

I leaned forward and I kissed him.

Chapter 8

His lips were cold but they were as soft as I remembered. Jack didn't move or do anything for the longest time and I started panicking when I started to realise what a terrible mistake I'd just made. I was about to pull away and sputter apologies for being so stupid and weird when I felt Jack slip a hand behind my neck and pull me closer.

He started moving his mouth against mine, and warm liquid poured into my stomach, making me feel fluttery and light. Somewhere in the back of my mind, I vaguely noted that Jack was kissing me back and it was the best thing that happened since we went on this Godforsaken trip. He nudged my mouth open and I titled my head to the side.

My breath hitched in my throat jumped as he deepened the kiss. It was sweet and warm and slow and we hadn't kissed in so long I had forgotten that Jack Marshall was an amazing kisser. It was so easy to slip back into our routine and forget where we were. My hands in knotted in his wet hair and his fingers lightly kneading the back of my neck. I wanted to kiss him until my lungs were screaming for air and the world felt too far away too be real.

I never got to do that since Jack let out a soft groan and in a split second, whatever spell had come over me shattered and I pulled back. My eyes were wide open as I scrambled away from him. He stared at me with the same gob smacked expression, his mouth was red and a little swollen from the kiss and it made me want to do kiss him again. I looked up. Callie was staring at her nails and Oliver's eyebrows were raised high as his gaze skipped between me and Jack. The awkward tension hanging in the air was so thick you couldn't cut through it.

Breathing hard, I pushed myself up and slicked my soaking hair back and out of my face.

"Uhm," I mumbled, trying desperately to regain my composure and not look like an idiot. I guessed from the weird way Jack was looking at me, and the way Callie was smirking like she knew a secret, I was failing terribly. "S-sorry," I said, I wasn't quite sure I was apologising to let alone why. "Yeah, sorry, uhm..."

The awkward silence returned, everyone kept staring at me and it made me want to jump into the lake and never come back. Thankfully, it didn't last long because Callie clasped her hands together and beamed at her brother, "Jack, are you okay?"

Jack seemed dazed and lost as he nodded his head. Oliver helped him stand up. His knees buckled and he almost fell over but Oliver had a secure arm around his waist and he'd placed Jack's arm over his shoulders.

"We thought you were goner," Callie said as she followed Oliver, who was guiding Jack to the large stretch of grass at the edge of the woods. When they reached it, Oliver slowly let go of Jack and sat him down. Jack grunted and rolled onto his back so he was staring up at the clear sky.

"I'm fine," He coughed, "you guys can't get rid of me that easily."

I stayed by the rocky shore of the lake, wanting to keep my distance from Jack just for a little while as I calmed myself down.

"Did I die?" he asked, "cause it kind of felt like I died."

Oliver shook his head, "no, Peryn pulled you out. You weren't breathing so she did some CPR shit and bam."

"Yeah, she did kind of save your life." Callie said.

I waited with baited breath for his reply.

"Oh," he said.

Oh? I'd just saved his life and all he could say was oh?

"Thank you," he said and he said it so quietly I almost missed it. He glanced over at me, his deep brown eyes soft and they were swimming with some raw emotion, I couldn't quite place. He looked like he was going to say something else but he was interrupted by his sister.

Callie grinned and ruffled his dark hair, "I'm just glad you're okay."

He batted her hand away with a frown.

"We should not have survived that fall," Jack said and coughed again, "it's a fucking miracle we didn't hit any rocks on the way down. I mean, the height of the waterfall times by the speed we were falling should have killed us. The impact would be like hitting a brick wall. "

"Yeah, well, try not to think about that," Oliver said as he sat down next to Jack.

He was rambling again, I could see the numbers and equations churning around his head as tried to work out the possibilities of us surviving something like that. A small smile tugged at my lips. It was kind of endearing.

"I mean the fall effects alone are lethal," he said, he was talking to himself more than anyone else, "just calculate the presence of debris at the base, and risk of being hit by other objects in the flow, the water at the base of the fall is extremely turbulent, with currents that can suck you under and keep you there for longer than you can go without air, and–"

"Jack," Callie said, already exasperated with his ramblings. She slumped down onto the grass, seating herself next to him. "Stop, I really don't want to think about it."

The three of them were now lying on the grass, soaked and shivering. Oliver rose so he was resting on his elbows, he waved at me, "yo Peryn, come join us. We need to rest."

I nodded, "yeah, okay."

My left leg was feeling odd, like I'd pulled a muscle but not quite. My limbs didn't feel like they belonged to me. I hobbled over to them, and I lay down next to Callie. I needed to keep a safe distance from Jack. The sun was now hanging high in the sky and shining directly down at the four of us. I sighed and I closed my eyes. I was cold and soaked to the bone so the beating heat was eagerly welcomed. Callie and Oliver continued talking but I wasn't listening. In the past six hours my body had been pushed to its limit by crazy bears, wolves and an inhumane amount of running.

The grass beneath me was soft and the sunshine was warm and soon enough I fell asleep.

I don't know how long passed when I woke up, the sun had dipped lower and Callie and Oliver were nowhere to be seen. I blinked, yawning as I pushed myself up so I was sitting up. I stretched my arms and arched my back, feeling the satisfying crack, I let my arms drop back down. I smiled, noticing that my clothes had all but dried. I touched my hair, it was probably a wild frizzy mess but it had dried too.

"You're awake."

My eyes snapped over to the familiar voice, and I felt my pulse rate speed up at the sight of Jack sitting a few metres away. He gave me a nervous smile as he nudged his glasses up onto his nose. I was surprised he hadn't lost them yet or at least broken them. Then again, Jack was probably the most responsible one in our little group.

"Where are Callie and Oliver?" I asked.

"Callie said she was cold, so I told them to collect some wood and build a fire," he replied, "they left about fifteen minutes ago."

"Those two don't know the first thing about building fires," I said.

"I know but it should be funny watching them try."

I laughed at the image of Callie and Oliver fighting over which sticks to rub together and who even get to rub those sticks. I looked up at the sky. If I closed my eyes, I could pretend I was in my back garden, sitting on the patio with a glass of cool orange juice as I soaked up the spring sun. We were quiet for a while, the only sound came from the wind rustling through the leaves and the birds singing in the trees.

"I miss you," Jack said, whispered more like, but I caught it and it made me freeze. It came out nowhere but at the same time, I knew it was coming. This whole trip had been stifled with the unsaid words from our break-up and I'd guessed that sooner or later it would all come spewing out. I just really, really hoped it wouldn't.

I closed my eyes and didn't say anything back. I could feel his gazw on me. He was waiting for my answer but I gave none. I couldn't.

"Peryn," he said.

I opened my eyes but didn't look at him, I kept my gaze on the grass beneath us. I frowned, "Yeah, I heard you."

"Well," he said and I could hear the frustration rising in his voice, "Say something."

My jaw clenched, refusing to respond. I had nothing to say to him. I felt as if it had all been said the day we broke up, so what did it matter now?

"Peryn," he said.

I tried to ignore him but he placed his hand on my shoulder and turned me to facw at him. His brown eyes were wide, beseeching but more determined than I had ever seen them. I knew Jack, I'd known since were seven years old and in that timehe hadn't changed. He was still the same stubborn kid who waited in line for eight hours for the latest Avengers comic. When Jack wanted something, he wouldn't stop until he got it and right now, he wanted me to talk.

"Peryn, for God's sake–"

I grit my teeth, my eyes closing for a split second before they snapped open and I glared at him.

"What the fuck do you want me to say, Jack?!" I said, my voice rising into a shout. "What? What the fuck do you want from me?"

He looked taken back for a moment, surprise flickering across his features. I shrugged his hand off my shoulder and pushed myself up so I could stand. Goddamn it. I brushed the dirt off my shorts and glanced around the area, hoping I would catch sight of Callie and Oliver. They should have been back with the wood by now, it shouldn't take this long.

"I want you to talk to me," he said in a tone you would reserve for a small child, "You've barely spoken to me since we broke." He sighed, "I mean, I, at least, hoped we would stay friends, y'know?"

Friends. Something about that word just made me want to throw something at him. I looked around for a rock, something that would hurt him as badly as he'd hurt me. It would have to be big enough to knock him out.

"Friends?" I stared at him, "you seriously expected us to be friends after you made out with Esther Townsend?"

Esther Townsend was this small, redheaded girl who'd had a crush on Jack since the freshman year. I think they would have already been dating if Jack hadn't had a crush on me since, well, since forever according to him. He'd told me that about a week after we'd started going out, and I'd laughed and kissed him because I couldn't believe he'd liked me for so long.

He pressed his mouth into a fine line for a second before he spoke, "I told you, I didn't make out with her."

"I fucking saw you!" I shouted, his calm only infuriated me further, "You know what, you're just the same as all the douchebag guys at our school and I can't believe I thought you were different!"

His eyes snapped up to look at me then and I knew I'd hit his weak point. He was looking at me and I mean really look at me, not just a quick glance filled with guilt. I saw the infuriating calm that had held him together crumble. He had the same expression he wore when he'd stumbled across a particularly difficult equation and he wasn't sure how to solve it. It was a look of fascination, frustration and confusion and the fact it was directed at me made my breath catch in my throat.

"I didn't want to kiss her!" he snapped, "How many times do I have to tell you this! She kissed me! She came over to mine because we were working on a project together for Chemistry and she said something about having crush on some guy for ages but I didn't know she meant me, so I tried to console her but she leaned forward and kissed me...and that's when you walked in!"

I'd heard the story a hundred times through voice messages and texts but I just couldn't get past that moment I'd walked into his bedroom and I'd seen Esther kissing him on his bed. He'd pulled away and when he saw me, his eyes had flew open. He'd called my name but I turned and just left, not wanting to hear any of his pointless excuses.

Jack shook his head and I could see the hurt swimming in his dark eyes, "You really think I would cheat on you? Peryn…Peryn, I've had a crush on you since we were six years old," he said, looking so sad it made my heart ache. "why…why, when I've just got the one thing I've always want-ed, why would I screw it up by kissing Esther Townsend of all people?"

I could feel my own resolve crumbling, "I-I don't know," I said, trying to keep my expression as stony as possible, "you're a boy, boys don't think."

He frowned, that steely determination snapped back into him, "You know I wouldn't! You know you're the best thing that's ever happened and you know I would never do any-thing to hurt you!" he said and I wasn't sure if I was imagining that quiver in his voice, "but we both know you'd been look-ing for any excuse to break up with me before Esther kissed me."

"What?" my eyes widened, "What the fuck are you talking about?"

"I'm talking about the fact that you were embarrassed to be dating me! I mean…I don't blame you," he sighed and glanced away, "have you seen yourself, Peryn? I never got why you liked me, it didn't make any sense. You're so…You're the most beautiful girl at our school…You're gorgeous and kind and funny and….and I'm just Callie Marshall's geeky brother."

I stared at him for the longest time, lost for words with my heart drumming hard in my chest. Jack refused to look at me, he kept his attention on a spot faraway.

"Jack," I said, managing to find my voice, "I wasn't embarrassed to date you, God...I..." I paused and took a deep breath. I'd hoped I would never have to admit this.

Something in my voice must have made him finally look back at me, because he said, "what?"

"I wasn't embarrassed because we were dating," I began, suddenly wishing the ground would open and swallow me up, "I...Damn it, I was embarrassed because I thought I wasn't good enough for you."

He blinked, "Wait...what?"

"I don't know," I said, "it's just...it's just that you get straight A's in all your classes and you have the highest GPA in school and all your friends are geniuses like you and...every time, I was with them I just felt so dumb. They kept saying how I was the last person they expected you to date, y'know because they thought you would go someone with a huge I.Q. like Esther Townsend or Reinette Thayer," I bit my lip, "and...and I'm nowhere near as smart or perfect as them."

The way he was looking at me then, it made me want to run and run and run until I'd couldn't run any longer. Jack took a step towards me, slowly like I was a wounded animal he didn't want to scare away but also like I was the answer to every difficult sum he'd ever faced. "Peryn, I–"

"Guess who caught not one, not two, not even three fish you bitches!" Oliver shouted out of nowhere, "but four fucking fish?! Callie tell them!"

Jack and I whipped around to see Callie and Oliver emerging from the woods. Callie shouted, "Oliver Odysseus Kaminski!"

"Damn straight!" Oliver grinned and Callie grinned back at him, "I caught four fucking fish guys! Four!"

It was then that I saw the fish Oliver was carrying in his hand, he proceeded to hold them up proudly. My eyebrows rose, "Jesus Christ...h-how?"

He shrugged like it was nothing, "Me and Callie were by the river, and I was washing my face when I noticed some movement in the water. It took me a second to realise they were fish and then I remembered this documentary I saw on Fox about noodling, so I just stuck my hands in the water and caught some fish!"

"And I gathered the wood!" Callie said, gesturing to the bundle of sticks she held under her arm. She laughed and imitated a poor Texan accent, "Yee-haw! We gon' feast tonight!"

Chapter 9

The fish was delicious. None of us had eaten since yesterday and we'd been running all day from bears and wolves so you could imagine just how tired and hungry we were. Once the fish had finished cooking, it was no surprise that the four of us practically inhaled the fish down.

Since Callie had gathered the wood and Oliver had caught the fish — which I couldn't stop thanking him profusely for because I, honestly, thought I would die of starvation in these Godforsaken woods — it was my job to the light the fire by rubbing the sticks together like my dad had taught me during our camping trips and Jack's job to actually the fish. He was able to set up a make-shift pit roast from branches and rocks, so he could properly cook the fish. The last thing any of us wanted was food poisoning.

It took a little over half-an-hour for the fish to be ready. In that half hour, the four of us just stared at the fish, the smell making our mouths water and stomachs grumble. When it was ready to be eaten, I bit into it faster than the speed of light. I didn't even care that some of the skin was burnt. None of us did. Jack said the lake was freshwater so we could drink some but there was no guarantee that it was completely safe. Me, Callie and Oliver were too thirsty to care, as soon as he said it was okay, we dived to the lake and slurped the water like a bunch of stray dogs. Soon enough, the sun had sunk far into the horizon and left the sky black and dotted with stars.

"We can't keep walking," I said, when we'd all finished eating. We'd agreed to save the rest of the fish for later because God knows we needed food. "It's too dark, and no way am I walking in the woods at night. That's just asking to get mauled to death by those freaky wolves."

Callie nodded in agreement, "Per's right, also, I'm really tired."

"Okay, but where are we going to sleep?" Oliver asked as he bundled up the remaining fish in some large leaves. I'd torn them from the small tree that sat on the edge of the lake.

We were all quiet for a few seconds. I looked around but it was hard to see when it so dark and not to mention, it was getting a little chilly.

"Here," I said, gesturing to the little campsite we had set up. We were all sitting around the fire, between the lake and soft patch of grass a few feet away. "I think the fire should keep the animals away but we can all take it in turns to keep the fire going and watch in case some wild animal comes for us, whilst the rest of us sleep."

"We're sleeping on the floor now?" Callie whined, "Like a bunch of homeless assholes?"

Jack glared at his sister, "Well, we wouldn't be sleeping on the floor like a bunch of homeless assholes if it wasn't for you."

She even had the gall to look surprised, "How the hell is this my fault?"

My eyes widened along with Jack and Oliver. I gaped at her, "Callie, we are all in this mess because you picked up Bosco, that bastard hitchhiker! It was your fault he stole your car!"

"That was Oliver's idea!" she said, pointing an accusing finger at the dark-haired boy who was still wrapping up the fish. "He told me to do it, he said it would be good karma!"

"I...I don't remember that!" Oliver spluttered, "and...and even if it was me, you were the one who stole that bear cub!"

"I thought it was alone!" she said, "I thought its mom abandoned it and...I...I gave it back! But you...no you just had to go and call the bear a little bitch!"

"That's because it was a little bitch!" Oliver cried.

Callie's eyes narrowed, "Kaminski, you heartless bastard, what —"

"Enough!" Jack shouted, making all of us jolt. We all turned to look at him. He sighed and rubbed either side of his head with his fingers. "Goddamn it...just...shut up, will you? You're going attract more wild animals if you don't shut up...whatever, I'm going to sleep, I can't deal with you guys anymore."

He lay down on the floor and turned onto his side so his back was facing us. Oliver and Callie went back to their argument, this time whispering in low, harsh voices but I kept looking at Jack. Our earlier conversation swirled in my mind, it played on constant repeat and his face, the way he'd looked at me after I'd told him I felt I was never good enough for me. I still couldn't believe he thought I was embarrassed of him.

Even before Jack and I started dating, I would always marvel at his intelligence and his serious determination in everything he did. Jack Marshall was probably the smartest person at James Wolfe Secondary, he was certified genius and I just knew that brain of his was going to change the world. Jack Marshall was the kind of person you found in history books two hundred years from now. Jude Sinclair had once told me I was the kind of person you would find plastered on some billboard advertising the swimwear. He then gave me that stupid grin he thought was charming and told me to thank God I was hot because not many people were that lucky.

I glanced at Callie and Oliver who were still arguing and sighed. "Go to sleep," I told them, "I'll keep watch."

Callie frowned, "are you sure?"

I nodded, "yeah."

I couldn't sleep anyway, my mind was buzzing with too many thoughts. It was better I stay up. A little time by myself would let me clear my head.

"Oh cool," Oliver said, linking his hands behind his head and lying down on his back.

Callie stared at me for a few seconds, looking unsure before she nodded and lay down next to Oliver. "Just wake me up when you're tired," she said.

"Okay."

It didn't take long for them to sleep, in fact they were both snoring within ten minutes and within twenty minutes, they had migrated towards each other so that they were snuggling. I stayed up for about an hour, or maybe it was two, I don't know but it was hard to keep track. I stayed up and looked at the midnight sky, my thoughts circling around Jack Marshall and everything that had happened between us. It wasn't until I yawned that I felt the weight of this horrible camping trip. I scooted over to Callie and nudged her awake. She grumbled something but didn't move, so I lightly patted her cheek.

"Huh? Wha?" she mumbled as she blinked awake. "Peryn? Is Winston back? Is my baby bear here?"

I shook my head, "no, Callie, it's your turn to watch."

She nodded as she slowly pushed herself up, "hm, yeah, okay."

I didn't like the idea of sleeping on the dusty floor, so I placed my head on Callie's lap and I fell asleep to the sound of the crackling fire and the feel of Callie running her fingers through my hair.

The next morning, I was woken up by the sound of Oliver singing in my ear and the sharp pain of Callie kicking my leg. I jolted and looked up at the them. They both grinned. I swear, throughout this trip they had morphed into more horrible version of Tweedledee and Tweedledum. Maybe it was the fact we'd been cut off from civilization and technology for nearly three days now. I heard that drove some people to insanity.

"Wha...What the hell?" I said, rolling over so I lay on my back, "what are you doing?"

"You wouldn't wake up," Callie shrugged.

"Dude," Oliver smirked, "You're, like, the heaviest sleeper."

I grumbled a string of insults as I pushed myself up. I yawned and stretched my arms until I felt some movement slip back into my limbs. I breathed in the spring air that had earthy scent of burnt wood and wild flowers blooming in the distance. Ignoring the fact that we were lost in a national park and completely screwed, it was a beautiful day. I had woken up just in time to see the sun rising in the east and light up the sky with streaks of pink and orange. I couldn't remember the last time I'd see a sunrise. In a big city like Vancouver, it was easy to get lost in the movements of everyday life.

"We need to keep moving," Jack said behind me.

I glanced back at him. He kept poking the dying campfire with a long stick.

"Do you even know where we are?" I asked.

"Sort of," Oliver said.

Jack said, "I broke my cellphone when we fell into the lake but I managed to fix it, it's water damaged so I can only switch it on for about a minute before it dies. I was able to check the map and it turns out we're actually closer to the town, we're about fifteen miles away now. We just need to keep going south, follow the river and we'll be okay."

"Oh thank God," I said. That must have been the first bit of good news I'd heard since we went on this trip. The river Jack was referring to spewed into a narrow lane from the large lake below the waterfall. It ran deep into the woods, twisting and turning throughout the national park until it met the North Pacific Ocean.

"Who's got the fish?" Jack asked.

Oliver raised his hand and said, "moi."

I saw that he had finished wrapping the last of the fish from last night in leaves. He had bundled them shut with a string he'd pulled from his tattered shirt. I glanced around at all of us and saw, all our clothes were dirty and ripped. To be frank, we all looked like shit.

"Okay, let's go," Jack stood up and stretched his back. He gestured for us to follow him, "It should take four maybe, five hours to get to Linbeach if we follow the Heward River, since it runs straight through the town."

I would ask how he knew all this but the answer was pretty obvious. The perks of being a genius like Jack Marshall meant that you had a photographic memory. All he had to do was see something once and he could remember it.

I hung back with Oliver as Callie jogged ahead of us to walk alongside her brother. We left the clearing surrounding the waterfall and stepped into the dense forest. The earthy smell was stronger here, the smell of wild flowers had gone and in its place was the smell of damp air and pine. The river was nearby, we could hear the rushing water as we walked through the sun dappled woods.

My gaze kept skipping to Jack. He has a somber expression and his answers were short and curt. I wondered if he was thinking about our argument. He probably was, Jack had a tendency to obsess over things and I bet he couldn't stop thinking about our argument either. That was why he hadn't made any eye contact with me since last night. I sighed. If the tension between Jack and I wasn't awkward before, it definitely was now. Everybody in the group could feel it, it was almost suffocating.

After about an hour of walking, we came to a deep gorge the river ran through. it must have been a fifty foot drop or more. We could see the river rushing between the rocky hills and the only thing that connected them was an old rope bridge that looked like it would fall apart any second. Did Jack expect us to cross that thing?

I glanced at Callie and Oliver, happy to find they all looked as freaked out as me.

"I know what you're thinking," Jack said, "but we have to get to other side if we want to follow the river."

"Isn't there another way?" Oliver asked, eying the gorge nervously.

"If there was, I would have thought of it," he said.

Oliver frowned, "Well, since it was your idea, you can cross it first."

I expected Jack to argue and maybe call Oliver a moron like he always did, but he just sighed. "Okay," he said, "whatever."

I blinked, surprised at his placated reaction. I caught a glimpse of his expression, it was as still as somber as ever but he looked tired more than anything, like he could sleep for a thousand years but it still wouldn't be enough. I had the sudden urge to kiss him and keep kissing him until he didn't look so beat.

I felt my heart creep into my throat as Jack stepped onto the creaky bridge, he clutched onto the rope and started to slowly walk across it. It wobbled slightly with each step he took. I didn't realise I'd been holding my breath until he reached the other end. He turned round to face us and gave us a thumbs up.

"It's okay!" he shouted, "come on, one person at a time and make sure you walk slowly!"

Callie, Oliver and I looked at each other for a few moments. When no one made a move, Callie gave me and Oliver pointed looks. She shook her head.

"Pussies," she said and stepped onto the bridge. Callie whistled as she walked across it with more ease and grace than Jack had, she didn't even seem the slightest bit bothered that she was walking on a rickety bridge fifty feet above a rushing river.

Oliver shook his head, "there is no way, I'm crossing that thing. It's a fucking death wish."

It seemed like me and Oliver were the only ones who understood just how unsafe that bridge was. I thought I heard a weird sound behind me, so I glanced back. My eyes narrowed as I peered into the woods. I was just about to look away and put down the noise to the wind or just my imagination when I saw a low figure emerge between some trees. I watched with baited breath as it crept out of the shadows and stepped into the morning light. I gasped.

"Oh my God," I whispered. "Oliver."

"What?" he turned around and followed the direction of my gaze.

"Get on the bridge," I told him.

"Holy shit," he said, "did...did it fucking follow us?!"

"Get on the bridge, Oliver," I said as I stepped backwards, keeping my eyes on the bear that crept out of the woods. It was eying us, like it was sizing up, seeing how good we would taste.

"No way," Oliver said, "no way, am I getting on that —" the bear roared, "I'm getting on the bridge!"

Callie glanced back, frowning because she wasn't even half away across the bridge. "What are you doing? Jack said one person at a time!"

"There's a bear!"

"A what —?" she cried and looked behind us. Her eyes widened, "Oh my God!"

"I know!" I shouted as I reluctantly stepped onto the bridge. I clutched onto the rope for dear life and moved as carefully but as I quickly as I could.

Callie grinned, "it's Patricia!"

I paused and looked at her, "Patricia? As in Winston the Bear's mother?"

Callie nodded, "yeah! I know it's her!"

"Stop talking and move!" Jack shouted from the other end of the bridge. "Do you want to get eaten?"

Behind me, I heard the bear, Patricia as Callie had named her, let out another roar. I looked back and saw her stalk towards the bridge. Oh God, she wasn't going to try and cross it, right? Callie had reached the end of the bridge, so it was just Oliver and I, which was a terrible idea because this thing could only support one person at a time.

"Oliver!" I snapped, "Go quicker!" The clumsy way he was walking was making the whole thing wobble and I felt like

I was a second away from tumbling over and into the river below. A fall from this height would probably kill me.

"Come on!" Jack shouted,

"Yeah!" Callie joined in, "keep going, you're nearly there!"

I frowned. It was easy for them to say, they were safe on the other side whilst me and Oliver were risking our lives on this Godforsaken bridge. My heart was beating so hard, I was afraid it would explode in my chest. I tried not to look down. I just concentrated on taking careful steps on the wooden boards of the bridge. I didn't look up when I heard Oliver hoot and holler about how he'd gotten across. Jack, Callie and Oliver soon started shouting for me to hurry up like a squad of terrified cheerleaders. I was literally a few inches from the Jack, who stood at the edge of the bridge, when my left foot crashed through one of the wooden boards and I stumbled. I screamed as the bridge started swaying left and right.

"Peryn!" Jack shouted. "Take my hand!"

I looked up at him. He'd leaned down and reached his hand out towards me.

I shook my head, too scared to move. "I can't!"

"Peryn," he said, his voice was softer this time, it matched his expression, "Peryn, it's going to be okay."

I took a deep breath and snapped left hand up to his. He latched on to it and holding onto the ropey railing of bridge with my right hand, I pushed myself up. Jack yanked me across the last bit of the bridge. We both stumbled and fell and for a horrible second, I thought we'd fallen into the gorge but when I opened my eyes, I was glad to find we'd landed on the grassy ground by the bridge. I lay on top of Jack, who had wrapped his arms around my waist. My heart stuttered in my chest. He stared up at me, breathing hard with his mouth slack and his deep brown eyes swimming with relief. We stared at each other for a few moments, marveling at one another and the fact I'd almost just died.

"Are you okay?" he whispered. His adam's apple bobbed as he swallowed.

I nodded since I didn't trust myself to speak. I watched, slightly entranced as the corner of his mouth quirked up- wards in a small smile that had butterflies swirling in my stomach.

"Uh, guys," Oliver said, snapping me out of the trance Jack had cast.

Callie said, "Patricia's crossing the bridge!"

Jack moved his arms off my waist and I clambered off of him. We both stood up and looked over to the bridge and much to our horror, Callie was right. The bear kept growling as it tried to cross the bridge. It was almost half way.

"We...we should just burn the bridge!" Callie said.

"Patricia!" Oliver shouted, "You little bitch!"

Callie punched his shoulder, "Shut the hell up! This is your fault! It probably wants you!"

"Well, it's not getting me," Oliver said as he shoved his hand in back pocket of his trousers and pulled out a gold-plated pocket knife, "I'm cutting this motherfucker down!"

Before we could say anything, Oliver rushed to the edge of the bridge and started cutting through the rope that were tied around the wooden posts on the edge of the rocky hill.

"Oliver!" I said, "Get back!"

He shook his head as he continued to furiously cut the rope. "No way!" he said, "no way am I letting that dumb bear tear me limb from limb and then feed me to its dumb bear baby!"

"Winston isn't dumb!" Callie said and she smacked the back of his head.

"Ow!" Oliver cried, "Can you stop hitting me?"

"Can you stop being a jackass?" she said.

He didn't answer. After another ten seconds of cutting, the lines of rope that held the left side of the bridge snapped off and it all flopped to the side. Patricia the Bear growled, she scrambled as the bridge swayed. Oliver instantly moved to the other side and started cutting.

"Wait, are you're going to kill it?" I said, my gaze skipping to the terrified animal.

"Oliver," Jack said, "if that bridge falls, that bear will die."

"Hell yeah!" Oliver said, "it's going to kill us!"

Callie's eyes widened, "No!"

Oliver grinned, "Yes!"

"Kaminski, you asshole! You can't kill Patricia!" she cried, "then Winston, won't have a mom! He'll be all alone!"

"That's the circle of life, baby!" Oliver said, still cutting away. I could see the rope giving way. If he kept going the bridge would collapse and Patricia would fall into the river.

"NO!" Callie screeched so loudly her voice echoed, "WE ARE NOT BEAR KILLERS!"

She lunged forward and knocked Oliver to the ground. Jack and I watched as the two rolled around on the floor. Callie kneed him in chest groin and smacked the pocket knife out of his hand. I took that moment to pick up the knife off the ground and throw it to Jack, who caught it with ease and shoved it into his jean pockets.

"Oliver," I said, "I've thrown your pocket knife in the gorge."

Oliver froze. Callie had gripped him in a tight headlock that had turned his face into a bright red. He looked up at me, "You...you what?"

"You were going to kill the bear," I said, "I had to!"

"The bear was going to kill us!"

"I don't care," I said, "we don't kill animals, Oliver, are you crazy?"

"Peryn that pocket knife cost three hundred dollars! It belonged to JFK!" he shouted as he pushed Callie off him and rushed to the bridge. "No! Stanley!"

Callie laughed, "Oh my God, you named your knife?"

Oliver threw her a glare, "So? You name random animals for no reason."

"Why do you have JFK's pocket knife?" I asked.

"That...that's...none of your business, Peryn!"

"Look," Jack said, "it's leaving."

The bear seemed to be freaked out by the swaying bridge, so it had retreated back to the other side. It stayed there for a while, just staring at us before it growled and turned around. It patted back into the woods. Once it was out of sight, I breathed a sigh of relief.

"Oh thank fuck," I breathed a sigh of relief once it was out of sight "we're safe."

Jack frowned, "Yeah. For now."

Chapter 10

"Wait, so your middle name is Odysseus?"

"Yeah, my dad's the professor of Classics at British Columbia," he explained, "he specialises in Ancient Greek literature and his favourite book of all time is the Odyssey, so, he wanted Odysseus to be my first name but luckily my mom talked him out of it."

"Oliver Odysseus Kaminski," I said and smiled, "it's actually pretty cool."

Oliver threw me a lopsided grin, "Thanks."

It was exactly forty-three minutes and twenty seconds since our encounter with Patricia the Bear. The four of us had eagerly continued walking because the more distance we put between us and that crazy bear, the better. We were still following the river, I could hear the rushing water a few feet away and every now and then, I saw glimpses of it between the bushes and the trunks of trees. Callie and Jack walked in front of us, they'd been discussing the daunting prospect of facing their mothers if they got back home. Callie was sure

Luna was going to ban her from driving until she graduated from high school and Jack was sure, Rosalie was not going to let him go to the San Diego Comic Con in July.

Oliver and I walked behind them, our conversation was less stressful. I'd never really talked to Oliver before this trip, mainly because I tended to avoid him since everybody knew Oliver Kaminski attracted trouble. I'd seen him around school and heard about his moronic escapades that landed him in detention or the principal's office at least twice a week. After I started dating Jack last year, around the second or third week of junior year, I saw more of him since he was best frients with Jack.

"What's your middle name then?" Oliver asked.

"I don't have one," I said, "My parents thought two was enough."

"You're lucky," he said, "my older sister's called Ithaca...It haca Arête Kaminski."

"Seriously?" I said with raised eyebrows, "wait... Ithaca is Odysseus' home and Arête is Poseidon's daughter right?"

Oliver looked impressed, "yeah, are you into Greek mythology or something?"

"Kind of," I said with a sheepish smile. We were currently learning about Greek mythology in World Literature and everything about it just fascinated me. "So, you're dad's a little obsessed."

He laughed, "Yeah, just a little."

I smiled at him and he smiled back. It was then that I wondered why I hadn't talked to Oliver Kaminski sooner. Yes, he could be an annoying idiot but so could Callie and I still loved her. I vowed, then and there, that if we ever got back home, I'd hang out with Oliver more.

Jack glanced back, his dark eyes skipping between the both of us for a moment before he looked away. I frowned and next to me, Oliver let out a small chuckle.

"What's so funny?" I asked.

Oliver shook his head, "Nothing."

I opened my mouth to ask him what was going on but I was interrupted by Callie.

"I can't do this anymore!" she said and stopped walking so she could lean against the trunk of a tree.

I sighed, "Join the club."

This entire trip had just been disaster after disaster and I didn't know how much of it I could take. I just wanted to go home. I missed my bed. I missed my parents, I missed mom and her frantic plans for the wedding. I missed my little sister, Dione and her excited squeals whenever a new episode of Fairly Odd Parents came on. God, I even missed Minnie and her trademark eye rolls. I just wanted to go back to Vancouver.

Jack looked at all of us, he must have seen how demotivated and tired we all were because he frowned and said, "We should take a break."

No one disagreed with him. We stepped out of the crowded woods and came to a grassy hill that overlooked the river. We all slumped down and we were quiet for a long while as we watched the river rush by before us. I looked up at the sky and let the mid-afternoon warm my skin.

Ignoring the fact that we were lost somewhere in Wells Gray Provincial Park and had nearly been killed more times than I could count, it was a beautiful day. I closed my eyes and listened to the sound of the frothing river and the birds singing in the trees and the pungent smell of wet earth and grass.

When I opened my eyes, I saw that Callie and Oliver had fallen asleep. Callie had her head on Oliver's lap and Oliver had his hands buried in her hair as he slept against the trunk of a birch tree. I wasn't sure who but one of them was snoring. Jack sat next to me with his elbows resting on his drawn-up knees as he looked down at the river. I watched, a little entranced as the wind swam by and ruffled his dark hair.

He looked at me then and my heart jumped in my chest.

"You know," he began softly, "I never thought I'd say this but...I actually miss Vancouver."

I chuckled, "Yeah, me too."

"But, um," he glanced away, back at the river.

I waited for him to continue speaking.

"Look, I know I messed up and I know you probably hate me but I really miss you and if this whole trip has taught me anything is that life is too short and unpredictable and it would be way better if life was too short and unpredictable with you," he said, the words spewing out in a heated rush. A red blush spread across his cheeks as he scratched the back of his neck.

My breathing stuttered as I stared at him with widened eyes. "Jack."

He nibbled on his lower lip and peeked up at me through his dark lashes. I opened my mouth to say something but no words came out. I looked at him and he looked back at me with those sad brown eyes that made my heart ache. I didn't say anything, I don't think I needed to. I just reached over, and slipping my hand in his, I wound our fingers together. I swallowed and leaned forward, or maybe he did. Our lips had just met in a warm, rushing haze of electric nerves and drumming hearts when Callie's laugh made us jump apart. If Jack's cheeks hadn't been red before, they were now.

I looked away from him and over to Callie, who was laughing at something Oliver had said. When had they woken up? It was then that I noticed Callie was holding something in her hands. I got up and walked over to them. She glanced up at me from her seat by the river bank.

"Peryn!" she said.

My eyes narrowed when I saw she had a bundle of dark red berries in her hand. I noticed she had the red juice from the berries smeared across her mouth and when she grinned at me, I saw her teeth were stained red as well.

"Callie, you can't just eat berries you found in the woods," I said, "do you know how dangerous that is? They could be poisonous."

"If they were poisonous don't you think I'd be dead?" She snorted, "c'mon, have some! Oh my god Per...they're so sweet!"

"Over there," she said, nodding her head towards the bushes near the large oak tree. I walked over to it and picked out a berry from the prickly bush. I peered closely at it, frowning when I realised it wasn't any kind of berry I'd seen before. They resembled wintergreens and cranberries, but they had a deeper colour to them, like darkened blood with a hint of purple. I frowned and racked my brain for any information that could help me identify them. I knew I'd seen them before, I just couldn't remember where.

It was then, as I watched Callie stuff more berries into her mouth and laugh hysterically that it dawned on me. A few summers back, I'd gone camping with the whole family and one day, Callum, my oldest brother had tried to eat some berries he'd found in the bushes. Dad had stopped him before they reached his mouth and thrown them into the lake.

"Callum, these are dangerous," he'd told my brother, "Never, ever eat them or you could land yourself in hospital."

She passed a few berries to Oliver and urged him to eat them. My eyes widened. I rushed over to him and knocked the berries out of his hand as roughly as I could.

"Hey!" Oliver cried, "wh-what the hell Peryn! I was going to eat that!"

"Don't eat them!" I snapped, "Those are Grenadine berries you idiot!"

He shrugged, "so?"

"So?" I stared at him, "they're really bad for you! They cause blurred vision, cramps, headaches, hallucinations and that's just the tip of the iceberg."

"Holy shit," Oliver said, he pointed to Callie, "you know she's had a shitload right? It's all she's been eating for the past ten minutes."

"Callie, spit those out!" Jack said, walking up behind me.

She looked more dazed than I'd ever seen her, her blue eyes were glazed over and she had this stupid, dreamy smile on her face. "But they're so delicious!" she grinned, revealing her berry stained teeth, "I'm, like, high on life!"

I stared at her, "You're high on berries."

"She's berry high," Oliver laughed, "get it? Berry high?"

Jack and I threw him pointed glares that told him how unimpressed we were with his little joke. He rolled his eyes and grumbled something about his comedic talents being wasted on idiots like us.

Callie burst out laughing and wouldn't stop until she was wiping tears from her eyes. "Oh my God! Berry high! Kaminski that's fucking amazing! I'm berry high!"

"See? Callie gets it," he grinned, looking way too proud.

"Callie isn't exactly in the best state of mind right now," I said.

Jack frowned at his sister. "Callie," he said, "give me the berries."

"No!" she shouted, taking a step back from us, "I need them!"

Before any of us could react, Callie turned and started running.

"Callie!" Jack shouted.

"You'll have to catch me first you assholes!" she laughed.

"Callie!" I shouted.

Jack and I took off after her, and behind me, I heard Oliver sigh and say, "Great, more running."

We followed her back into the woods. It wasn't hard because she was ridiculously loud and kept cackling like some sort of crazed witch.

"Callie!" I shouted, "Damn it! Stop!"

We clambered up a rocky hill in our efforts to catch Callie. I pushed past the thick foliage, wincing every now and then when I felt a branch snap against my leg or something prickly dig into my back. It was just darkness and bushes for several moments before light flooded us and the heavy wilderness seemed to give way to fresh air and open skies.

My jaw nearly dropped when I saw where we were.

"Holy shit," Oliver said.

"Am I seeing things or is this a highway?" Jack asked.

I shook my head, "you're not seeing things."

We were standing at the edge of a highway with dozens of cars zooming past us every few seconds. I grinned. I never thought I would be so happy to see a highway. I turned when I saw a flash of blonde in the corner of my eye. Callie had paused to stare at the highway like the rest of us. I took the opportunity to run over to her, she saw me and was about to run but I leaped forward and tackled her to the ground.

We both grunted and rolled around on the muddy floor as we grappled for control.

"Callie!" I said, "give me the damn berries!"

"NEVER!" she screeched.

Seeing no other choice, I elbowed her in the ribs. She let out a surprised scream and I slapped the berries out of her hand. I saw them roll down the steep hill and into the trees and thick bushes.

"No!" she cried, pushing me off of her and reaching her hand over to where the berries had gone. "No!"

I sighed and pushed myself up. I brushed the dirt off my shorts, which was pointless because they were tattered and practically caked in mud.

"C'mon, Callie," Jack said as he helped her up. He had an arm around her waist and clung onto the arm she had slung around his shoulders. He frowned, "how many of those berries did you eat?"

Callie shrugged and giggled, "So, so many...but bro, don't worry, I've never felt better."

"Guys," Oliver said. We looked over at him. He stood at the edge of the road with his thumb raised. "We can try and get picked up."

"Oliver, no one is going to stop and pick us up," Jack said, "Have you seen us? Not only do we look homeless, but we look like maniacs. No normal person is going to-"

A car honked and we saw that the sound belonged to a black SUV. For a second, I thought it would pass us but it slowed down as it came to a stop before Oliver.

Oliver gave us a smug look, "Uh, sorry...what were you saying, Jack?"

Jack glared at him. I stepped forward so I could get a better look inside the car. The tinted windows wound down to reveal a grey-haired woman in the driver's seat. She looked to be in her mid-to-late forties with her ashy hair pulled back in a tight bun and she wore a pleasant enough smile as she looked at the four of us.

"Aw, are you poor things lost?" she asked in a sweet voice.

Oliver nodded, "yeah, look, it would be a major help if you could drop us off at the nearest town...which is...which is what, Jack?"

"Linbeach," Jack said.

"Yeah, Linbeach."

"Oh, oh of course!" she said, "I can't leave you kids out here by yourselves, it ain't safe, there's some dangerous animals round these parts."

I smiled, "oh thank you so much!"

"No problem!" she said and chuckled, "anything for fellow Canadians! I don't mind taking you guys to Linbeach, you need to get home, don't you?"

Oliver and I nodded. Oliver opened the back passenger door open and hopped into the car. I was about to do the same, when Jack grabbed a hold of my wrist. I glanced back at him, "What?"

He frowned, "Peryn, I'm not sure about this."

"Jack," I sighed, feeling too tired to argue with him, "I really wanna go home at this point."

"And so do I, it's just..." his eyes flicked over to the woman, who was now talking to Oliver about something, "I've got a really bad feeling about this."

"Callie's had way too many of those berries and she needs to see a doctor," I said, "the sooner the better. We can't stay in these woods any longer, we might die."

He glanced at his sister, her head had lolled onto his shoulder as she mumbled nonsense, and then back at me. He didn't seem happy about it, his mouth pressed into a fine line as he reluctantly nodded. I smiled and leant forward so

I could press a kiss to his cheek. The grimace melted from his face and in its place was a soft, dazed look that made my smile widen into a grin. I stepped into the back seat with Oliver. Jack pushed Callie in after me and he went to sit in the front with the woman.

Once we were all in, the woman smiled and started driving down the highway.

"And off we go!" she said.

Chapter 11

Jack and I started dating about a month and a half after I'd ended things with Tyler Wright. Callie had it in her head it was because of Jack but it wasn't. Truth is, things with Tyler hadn't felt right for a while but I kept holding onto the hope that it would get better. Tyler was a good guy, we got along and he treated me well but at some point in the summer before junior year, we just lost that spark. So, sometime in mid-July, I broke up with him. It wasn't heartbreaking or sad, to be honest, there had been a flash of relief in his eyes. We'd hugged, smiled and promised to stay friends. We still are, sort of. If we see each other in the hallway or in class he'll wave at me or I'll wave at him and we'll get back to our lives.

I still don't get how Jack and I came to be, all I remember is one day he went from beings Callie's geeky brother to being cute, smart Jack Marshall who made my heart pound and my days feel brighter. We were good together, everything felt different him, everything felt right.

I smiled as I glanced at the back of Jack's head. He was fiddling with his cellphone, he'd been trying to make it work properly since we fell into the lake yesterday.

We'd been driving for about twenty minutes and I sat in the back with Callie and Oliver. I stared out of the window, too tired to really pay attention to where we were going. I let the cars and the thick lines of trees pass by me in a blur. I couldn't remember the last time I actually sat in a seat this plush. God. It felt so nice to sit in somewhere that wasn't rigid and dirty. I was just so glad this whole ordeal was over. As soon as we got to Linbeach, we'd call home and one of our parents would come to pick us up. Yes, they would be pissed (I knew for a fact my mom was going to have a heart attack) but at least we would be back home. I couldn't wait to have a shower and wash off all this grime and dirt I'd accumulated in the last couple of days. Oh, and sleep in an actual bed instead of the hard ground. And oh my God, Wi-Fi and television and civilization instead of never-ending trees and wild animals. I never thought I would miss Vancouver so badly.

Callie dropped her head onto my shoulder and sighed. She sat between Oliver and I and kept alternating on who she slept on. I glanced over at her. She was still in that weird drug-fueled haze from the berries and every now and then she would say something nonsensical.

"Mrs Puff was a bitch," she mumbled against my shoulder. See, like that. She shook her head, "I mean, all SpongeBob wanted to do get that driving license, like...like what was her problem?" Callie's eyes widened, she seemed genuinely stressed by it, "Just 'cause her life was empty and aimless didn't mean she had to take it out on that poor yellow sponge."

"Oh my God," Oliver laughed, "You've lost your mind. Aw man, if my cellphone was working I would totally record this. You sound insane."

She sat up straight and looked at him, her eyes narrowed as if she was trying to figure out who he was. She pouted, "Kaminski? Is that you?"

"Yes, my dear. It's me," He grinned, wide and bright, "Your one and only."

She giggled, "Aw Kaminski! You wanna...know...you wanna know something?"

His grin remained as he cocked an eyebrow. "What?"

She leaned into him until her chest was pressed against his side and his grin faltered. "Don't tell anyone this but..." she lowered her voice to a whisper, "but I think you're kind of hot...I mean...have you seen your jawline?" she leaned back a little so she could run a finger across the very jawline she admired so much, "and...and I actually think you have a good body underneath but I don't get how since you skip gym class...and oh my God, you're such a good singer...I have to see your band perform sometime cause..." she imitated a gun with her hands and pretended to blow her brains out, "dude....you're so good."

At this point everyone in the car had tuned into Callie's ramblings.

"Did...did I mention you're hot?" Callie said with furrowed eyebrows.

Oliver's eyes had widened along with mine. "Yeah, you mentioned it."

"Which is weird 'cause you're not my type and it's sad because...because you're really cute and you can sing and you make me laugh but I can't date you y'know?" she said, her words became a little bit slurred, "No, like, offense or whatever but you're too short. Do you know how tall I am, Kaminski? I'm five foot ten, and I'm pretty sure you're like five foot six –"

"Five foot seven," he cut in.

"–and you know what that means? That means you would have to go up on your tip toes to kiss me or I would have to lean down or whatever and that's just awkward...I don't want that for us. Actually...you know what? Your height doesn't bother me that much, it's just, well –" She hiccupped, "I told Peryn I'm giving up on boys, which is exactly what I'm going to do. I'm just going to focus on myself this year 'cause like...like no offense or whatever but boys are trash..." she hiccupped once more and let out surprised giggle, "also and also you're...you're like in love with Peryn's cousin or whatever so–"

"What? I'm not in love with Ruby," Oliver chuckled but the redness spreading across his cheeks said otherwise.

Callie leaned back and laughed. Oliver sighed, he seemed relieved that she'd stopped pressing her boobs against him.

"Dude, you're so in love with her...I mean the whole reason you came to this camping trip is because you thought she'd be here." She grinned at him, "which is why we can't date. You're into Ruby and Ruby's into you so –"

Oliver's eyes widened once more, "Ruby's into me?"

Callie punched his shoulder and he yelped, "Will you stop interrupting me? Damn, let me get a word in edgewise, Kaminski. I'm trying to tell you something important–"

"Callie, what the hell are you doing?" Jack asked from the front seat. He leaned forward out of his seat and looked back at us.

"She's molesting me, man," Oliver said as Callie placed a hand on his shoulder. He batted it away and she pouted.

Jack frowned, "leave him alone, Callie."

"Why?" she whined.

"Because you're being creepy," I said, "we told you not to eat those berries."

She looked away from Oliver and her blue eyes flicked between Jack and me for several seconds. A smile shaped her lips as she bobbed her head. She placed her hand on Jack's cheek and her other on mine, "Y'know...I'm so, so, so, so happy you guys are back together."

"We're not back together," Jack and I said in unison. We froze and looked at each other, something like disappointment flickered in his dark eyes. I could almost feel the question hanging in the air between us. Why not?

"Yes, you are!" Callie patted our cheeks, "I mean, you have to be! You're...you're Jack and Peryn! If you two don't work then...then I'm gonna lose all hope! Peryn, do you have any idea how long Jack's liked you? Forever! For as long as I can remember he's been mooning over you and –"

Jack reached forward and slapped a hand over her mouth. He glared down at her, "Callie, for the love of God, shut up."

Her eyes narrowed and he snatched his hand back with a high pitched squeak.

"Oh God, ew, Callie, you licked my hand!" he said, his lips peeled back in disgust. "Gross."

Oliver started laughing again, "Holy shit, Callie...Callie, oh my god, we have to get you on those berries more often." He looked at me, "Hey, Peryn, what're they called again?"

"Why? So you can drug my best friend?" I said.

"O-o-oh, now drug is a strong word–"

"You kids alright back there?" the woman cut in with a smile, her gaze found us in the rear-view mirror.

Callie closed her eyes as she cocked her head to the side and grinned, "We're great! Thank you!"

I had almost forgotten she was there. She'd told us her to call her Flo Jo. It sounded like an absurd rap name but she said it was short for Florence Josefine. I looked out the window to see if we were anywhere near Linbeach but I was confused to find Flo Jo was driving down a narrow lane lined by high hedges on both sides. I told myself it was probably a short cut to Linbeach but that explanation went down the toilet when a pair of extensive iron gates came into view. They creaked open for the car and ahead, there was a modest farm house sitting atop a small hill. I glanced back in time to see the iron gates shut behind us.

"Wait, aren't you taking us to Linbeach?" Jack asked.

"Of course honey, it's just that the car's engine isn't sounding right and I'll need to take a look at it," she said, "you don't want to be breaking down in the middle of the highway now you do?" She came to a stop before the house and killed the engine, "It won't take long, whilst I take a look at it, you guys can rest and get something to eat. My husband will fix you up something nice. He makes the meanest apple pie."

Callie clapped her hands and I jerked. "Oh my God! I love apple pies!"

"Don't worry, I got just the thing to help your sister," she said as she pushed the door open and hopped out of the car, "it'll wash those berries right out of her system."

I opened the door and stepped onto the pebbled ground. I helped Callie out. She still couldn't walk properly, she kept stumbling, so I snaked an arm around her waist, pulled arm over my shoulders and let her lean against me as we headed to the house.

"Apple pies," Callie giggled, "hey, hey, Per? Have you seen American Pie? There's this scene where the guy gets an apple pie and sticks his–"

"Aw, gross," Oliver scrunched his nose up as he fell into step beside us, "that's the last thing I wanna think about when I'm eating that pie, Callie."

Jack was the last one to come out of the car. He paused and looked around, his eyes darting up to the house, to the horses in the distance and the gates behind us. "Jack," I said, when he turned to me, I waved him over, "C'mon."

There was a slight frown on his lips. He walked with a nervous energy as he headed over to us. Flo Jo opened the door and stepped aside to let us in. The hallway was heavy with the smell of cinnamon and leather. Flo Jo shut the door as the four of us looked around. A staircase stood at the end of the hallway and spiraled up to the second floor. Flo

Jo led us to the first door on the right, which turned out to be a small but cozy living room. There was a large bay window that looked out into the driveway and the endless green hills in the distance. The floral patterned sofas faced the fireplace and above that was a rather unnerving portrait of Steve Buscemi. He had two sets of eyes and his skin was a pale, sickly green but I was pretty sure it was Steve Buscemi.

Jack and Oliver looked just as creeped out by the painting.

"What the hell...?" Oliver mumbled.

Flo Jo noticed us staring and smiled, "Crud painted that, he's quite the artist."

"Who's Crud?" Jack asked, glancing away from the painting.

"My husband," she said, "Listen, why don't you kids make yourself at home?"

"Wait," I said as I led Callie to the sofa nearest the window and set her down. I turned to Flo Jo, "Wait, could we use your phone? We really nearly to call our parents to come get us."

Flo Jo shook head. "Oh I'm sorry darling but the phone lines have been down for a couple of days, damn storm wrecked it," she said, "but don't worry, as soon as I check my engine, I'll take you kids to Linbeach. It won't be long. Until then, just sit down and relax, Crud will be out with the apple pie in five minutes."

She gave us another tight smile and left the room.

"Flo Jo and Crud?" Oliver snickered, "Worst rap group ever. I won't be buying their album anytime soon."

He slumped down on the sofa next to Callie, who was already half asleep. He poked her cheek and she groaned, lazily batting his hand away. Jack grabbed me by my arm and pulled me to the side.

"Peryn," he said, his face etched with worry, "I have a really bad feeling about this place. Am I the only one freaked out by these people? For God sake, who has a huge painting of Steve Buscemi in their living room? That's not normal."

Even as he said this I could feel Buscemi's two sets of eyes staring down at us and I had to admit it was creepy.

"Okay, so, this place is a little weird–"

His eyebrows rose, "A little?"

I frowned. He was going to have a panic attack if he didn't calm down. I placed my hands on Jack's shoulders and looked him in the eye. I gave him my most reassuring smile.

"It's okay," I said, "we have some apple pie, she checks the engine and we go to Linbeach. If she doesn't do this in the next hour, we leave okay? You said yourself, Linbeach isn't too far."

Before he could say anything, I leaned forward and pressed my lips to his forehead. I smiled and kissed him on the mouth this time, short and sweet and enough to send butterflies racing in my stomach. Jack looked at me with so many stars in his eyes, it made me feel beautiful.

"Y'know," he said when I pulled away to look at him, "if you think kissing me is going to stop me from worrying about this creepy place then you're right."

I laughed, "I thought so."

On the sofa, Oliver made gagging noises. "This isn't a Nicholas Sparks novel," he said, "you guys don't have to get all smushy and yucky, and if you do, please do it at least three hundred miles from my vicinity."

Jack chuckled, "Oliver, shut up."

Just then, a short, chubby man in baggy jeans and a knitted sweater appeared in the doorway. He carried a pair of apple pies and four glasses of milk on a tray. The smell of apple pie, sweet and promising, filled the room and my stomach grumbled. I vaguely noted that the man was Crud and then I vaguely hoped his name wasn't really Crud.

"Who wants pie?" Crud said, grinning at all of us.

Oliver shook Callie awake.

"Huh? Wha– what's happening?" she said, bleary-eyed as she glanced around the room. "Is Patricia back? Winston... Winston, baby, are you here?"

"No, Callie," Oliver said and shook her once more, "snap out of it, the pie is here!"

Her eyes widened as she sat up straight, "Pie? Oh, pie."

Crud set the tray on the low coffee between the sofas and clasped his hands together, "Enjoy! Flo Jo said a little pie might cheer you up whilst she goes to check the engine."

I reluctantly pulled away from Jack and went to sit down on the sofa with Callie and Oliver. He soon followed and we all moved up to make space for him. Oliver reached for the pie and I quickly slapped his hands away. He winced and glared at me, "What the hell, Peryn?"

"Don't use your bare hands, you animal," I said, "there's three other people eating, God knows where your hands have been."

"Same place as yours," he said.

"All the more reason to use cutlery and a knife."

He rolled his eyes, "Whatever."

As soon as I cut the pie into equal pieces, we all grabbed out shares with the spatula and dug into the sweet, sweet, delicious pie. My eyes nearly rolled into the back of my head at how good it tasted.

Callie grinned up at Flo Jo's husband, "Oh thank you, Crap!"

Oliver nearly spat out his drink and I almost choked on the pie. Jack just bit lip to stop himself from laughing.

"It's Crud," Crud said, looking mildly offended, "Crud."

She smiled pleasantly, "Oh, isn't that what I said?"

Crud just stared at her for a moment. "Right, I'm going to see how Flo Jo is doing with the car, you kids enjoy the pie, I'll be right back."

As soon as he left the room, Jack, Oliver and I burst out laughing whilst Callie ate her pie like nothing had happened.

"Holy shit, Callie," Oliver said, "We seriously have to get you on those berries more often."

"Callie," I chuckled, "you can't call a grown man Crap."

"Well, a grown man shouldn't call himself Crud," Jack said.

"Guys," Callie said, staring at her hands like she'd just discovered them, "I don't feel too good."

I glanced at her, "That's what you get for eating random berries you find in the woods."

She wiggled her fingers and gasped a little, "No...like, my hands, they look weird."

Jack, Oliver and I watched in fascination as she continued to marvel at her hands. She had a slack jaw as she touched her nose, lips and eyes.

"Callie," Jack said, "What are you–"

Her eyes fluttered shut as she swayed to the side and passed out on my lap. I gasped and started shaking her shoulders but she didn't wake up. "Oh my God," I said, "Callie? Callie!"

Jack leaned over me and patted her cheek, his eyes had gone as wide as mine and Oliver's. "Callie!" he said and slid two fingers onto the side of neck. He shoulders sagged in relief, "It's okay, she's alive."

"What's wrong with her?" Oliver asked as he set his pie down.

"I don't know," Jack said, frowning as he checked the pulse on her wrist, "She's breathing, which is good."

"Oliver, go get Flo Jo and Crud, all those berries she ate might have finally caught up with her."

Oliver nodded and stood up. He started walking to the door but he came to a sudden stop by the fireplace. He frowned as he clutched the edge of the mantel piece.

"Fuck," he hissed.

"Oliver?" I said.

"I can't..." Oliver whispered. He stared at the ground like it was a great shark waiting to swallow him. "I can't feel my body...Dude, what the hell?"

"Oliver?" Jack said, rising up from his seat.

Oliver gasped and started clawing at the air, his arms flailed everywhere and he ended up hitting the long black vase on the mantelpiece and knocking it over onto the floor. It smashed and split in dozens of fractured pieces. We all froze as we stared at what had been in the vase.

"Am...Am I seeing things," Oliver asked, "or are those teeth?"

"Oh, you're hallucinating alright," Jack said, his eyes trained on the hundreds of teeth that split from the vase, "but not about the teeth."

My jaw dropped, "Please tell me they're not human–"

Oliver's knees buckled and he collapsed with a dull thud, he just missed landing on the mound teeth by an inch.

"Oliver!" Jack and I shouted.

Jack tried to take a step forward but he tripped and stumbled onto the floor. He couldn't pick himself up so he rose onto his knees and glanced over at me. He placed a hand on his chest, his breathing had turned ragged. The glazed look in his eyes freaked me out.

"Peryn, listen, the pie..." he said in a dark voice, "the pie... they put something in the pie."

"What?" I said and looked down at the pie we had all devoured in less than five minutes. I heard a thud and I looked up to find Jack had passed out like Callie and Oliver.

I swallowed. My heart started pounding in my chest as fear gripped me, icy and sharp and I wanted nothing more than to run. I opened my mouth to scream but I froze as a deep mistiness washed over me. It clouded my mind and numbed my body. The room seemed to widen, everything was too far away to be real. Even my hands. I stared down at them with horror, human flesh replaced by spaghetti and meatballs.

"Jack," I said as the room began to spin and spin and my eyes drooped shut.

The haze became too strong to resist, so I let myself be pulled down into the darkness.

Chapter 12

All I wanted was a nice camping trip with my best friend for a couple of days. That's it. I didn't ask for any of this. Yet, here I am, on this fine spring evening. The sky is clear, the moon is full and it would be pleasant if it wasn't for the fact I was about to die. I'm not even trying to be dramatic.

My head is pounding. It feels like there are a thousand hammering drums in my head that will never end. My throat is parched and every time I try to swallow it's like I'm eating sandpaper. It's not the hefty fire that crackles and pops ominously before me or the weird shrieking noise that's getting louder and closer with each passing second or even the fact that my once long black hair that fell to my elbows has been cut so it now barely brushes past my jawline. No, the thing that catches my attention first and foremost is the fact that my back is against a pole and my arms and legs have been tied securely to it with a rope.

"Peryn," says a raspy voice belonging to my best friend.

I look over at her, her once long blonde hair has been hacked away too, leaving a badly cut bob and like me she's been tied to a long metal pole.

"Hi, Per," she stares at me with wide eyes, "Can...you...Can you hear the birds singing?"

"Are you still hopped up on those berries?" I ask, she giggles and I frown.

"Oh wow, the night is...so pretty," she giggles again, her head swaying a little.

She's tied between her brother and his best friend who've also been fixed to the poles. They're both unconscious, I start praying for them to wake up soon.

"Wait," she says all starry-eyed, "can you see them?"

"See what?"

"The fairies," she whispers, "they're so pretty!"

Fear has fully settled in, clawing away at me as I see the dark figures of our captors coming closer and closer. How the hell did this happen? This was supposed to be a pleasant and peaceful camping trip. We were supposed to be spending five days camping in the wilds surrounded by nature, not five days of running for our lives from a crazy bear, rabid wolves and almost dying in a lake. How did it turn into such a horror fest? I'm exhausted, I'm hungry, my clothes are ripped and dirty, I have bruises in places I didn't even know you could get bruises, I haven't slept for forty-eight hours, and I'm pretty sure that angry bear is still stalking us.

"Oh my God," I breathe, frantically trying to undo the ropes but no matter how I hard I try they won't come off. It's no use, they've really knotted it tightly. It's beginning to cut the circulation in my hands and legs.

The sound of footsteps approaching pulls me out of my thoughts. The flickering light of the fire makes the duo look even more sinister. They step into the light of the fire and my jaw drops when I realise who the creepy pair are.

"You!" I gasp as I stare wide eyed at them, "you bastards!"

Flo Jo and Crud are wearing long white robes and a lot of wooden jewelry. I take in the long sticks they're carrying, the hats that look like – what I hope aren't real – deer skulls and the white swirling lines drawn onto their faces. This should bother me, this should really worry me but I've seen and done so many weird things these past few days that nothing seems to faze me anymore. This, I realize with horror, has become normality.

"What the hell is wrong with you people?" I ask, "You need help! Who does this?"

"Be quiet!" Flo Jo snaps.

"This evening!" Crud screeches as he raises the stick in the air, "this evening your bodies and souls shall be sacrificed to the great moon spirit above!"

I'm starting to think that maybe this camping trip was a bad idea after all.

"Oh great moon spirit above!" Flo Jo claps her hands and starts rubbing them together, "Accept our first human sacrifice and bless our lives with your mighty power!"

Crud reaches into his robe and pulls out a long dagger, the sharp metal glints in the moonlight. He passes it to Flo Jo with a curt nod. She pulls the knife to her lips and whispers something and then kisses it. Crud takes her staff and watches as she takes slow, mechanical steps towards me. My heart pounds so loud in my chest I'm afraid a heart attack is coming.

"No, no, no, no," I shake my head, "Stop it!"

"Relax child," she whispers, "I'm only going to slit your throat and drink your blood."

"You're fucking insane!" I scream. I shake and wiggle but the rope has been tied so tightly it's almost impossible.

I turn my face away and squeeze my eyes shut as she raises the dagger and –

A deep, growling roar cuts through the silence and we all freeze. Flo Jo's head snaps back and forth as she tries to find out where the noise came from. The roar sounds again, it echoes in the night and makes Crud jolt behind her.

"Honey, go check what that is," she says, "I think it's coming from the garage. It might be those damn wolves again."

Crud's sweaty face has turned ashen. "Uh, wolves? Honey, I don't think –"

"Go!" she hisses at him.

He jolts again and takes off running down the lane, disappearing into the darkness. Flo Jo huffs and turns back to me. She raises her knife and then, suddenly, comes to a stop. Her eyes slide shut as her knees buckle and she collapses face first into the hard ground. I look up, my heart in my throat, to find Jack standing before me, holding a shovel in his hands and wearing the same shocked expression as me. He takes his hardened gaze away from Flo Jo's unconscious self and glances at me. The steely look in his eyes melts away.

"Peryn," he says, dropping the shovel and stepping closer to me. "Are you okay?"

I nod and blink away the tears. Relief is a wave of warmth as Jack places a hand on my cheek. He leans forward and gives my forehead a quick kiss before he walks behind me. For a short, terrifying second I think he's run off somewhere but then I feel his hands tugging at the knots of the rope. I sigh. It takes longer than I would like but he soon cuts through the rope with something sharp and frees my hands and feet. I let out a long sigh as I step away from the pole.

"Where did you get the shovel?" I ask as I rub my wrists, their red raw from the rough rope.

"There's a small hut back there," he nudges his thumb to the patchy trail behind him, "They got all these weird tools. Do you know they have bayonet?"

I nod and look over at his pole and see the ropes lying on the floor.

"Okay but how did you get out?" I ask as he heads over to Callie.

"This," he says, waving a gold-plated pocket knife, "I had it in my back pocket."

I say, "Oliver's pocket knife?"

"No...no, that's JFK's pocket knife guys," Callie whispers like it's a great conspiracy, "Kam-Kaminiski isn't supposed to have that, it's like an American historical artifact or some-thing. Y'know...y'know it's on the market for like fifteen thou-sand dollars? I...I don't even get how he got it...Kaminski's so, so shady, guys like what the hell? I mean, what's he doing with a dead president's pocket knife?"

Callie continues to ramble on as Jack starts cutting into the ropes tied around her. I walk over to Oliver who is still passed out against his pole. The firelight flickers across him, deepening the shadows on his face and giving him an ominous look. We have to be quick. Crud is going to be back any second.

"Oliver," I pat his cheek gently. "Oliver."

He doesn't move, his head just lolls to the side.

I pat his cheek again. Nothing. I frown and I smack him so hard across the face it leaves red mark on his cheek. His eyes snap open. He gasps, his hazel eyes flitting all over before they land on me.

"P-Peryn?" he splutters, "What the hell is going on?"

"Oh you know, the usual," I say, "We got drugged by a creepy married couple who want to sacrifice us to some great moon spirit."

He just stares at me, "What?"

I walk behind him and start tugging at his ropes but it's useless. I look over at Jack, he's freed Callie from the pole and is now holding her up since she's still feeling the effects of the berries. They won't be fully out of her system for another three hours. I wonder how we're all going to get away quickly with Callie so intoxicated on those berries. I'm really starting to hate camping. Oh, why did I think this would ever be good idea?

"Jack, give me the knife," I say.

He holds onto Callie with one arm on her waist and digs into the back pocket of his jeans with his free hand. He pulls out the knife and chucks it to me. I catch with it ease and turn back to Oliver. I cut through the ropes around his shoulders, then the ones on his hands and finally, I bend down and cut the ones around his feet. Oliver stumbles away from the pole with a long sigh.

"Is that mine?" he asks, spotting the knife in my hand.

"Uh, yeah," I say and hand it over to him.

"Oh my God," he grins, turning the pocket knife over in his hands, "Stanley, my baby."

Callie's eyebrows draw together as she watches him, "You're so weird."

Oliver ignores her and continues to shower the pocket knife with love.

"We need to go now," Jack says, "Now."

"Jack, look...I'm fine," Callie says, prying herself from him.

He says, "Are you sure?"

"Yeah, I'm good," she says, taking a deep breath, "I feel weird but...I'll be fine."

She wobbles for the first couple of steps and despite the small limp in her walk, she's fine. I look around and see that the light from the fire shows a pathway between a pair of great oak trees.

"Let's go then," I say.

We stay close together as we start walking down the path. Callie comes up beside me and slips her hand in mine. I squeeze her hand and she seems to relax a little. The gravel crunches beneath our feet and in the distance, there is the sound of owls hooting and crickets chirping. It would be pitch black if it wasn't for the moonlight filtering through the trees and illuminating the way. Everything has an eerie glow this time of night. It feels like there's something hiding in every corner, waiting to pounce.

"What time is it?" I ask.

Oliver glances at his wristwatch, "it's three in the morning."

As we keep on walking the trees and the thick foliage gives way to open space and the path becomes steeper downhill. Below, we see the farm house, bathed in moonlight. Jack's eyes light up and I follow his gaze, wondering what he's seen. That's when I spot the black SUV sitting in the driveway and I grin.

"C'mon," Jack says, as he starts jogging downhill.

He comes to a screeching halt when a figure jumps out of the bushes and into the moonlight. It takes me a second to realise it's Crud and he's holding a shotgun in his hands. He points it squarely at the four of us.

"I don't know where you kids think you're going," Crud says, taking a step forward, "but it's the wrong way."

Jack opens his mouth to say something but a great, rumbling roar cuts him off. I gasp. It's the same roar from earlier. Crud looks around panicked, aiming his shotgun at the sky, at the trees, anywhere and everywhere as he tries to pinpoint where the sound came from.

Oliver the takes opportunity to chuck his pocket knife straight at him. Crud turns just in time to let it smack him right in the eye. He screeches and the shotgun falls to the floor as he goes to cover his eye. Crud glances down at his hand, there's splotches of blood smeared across it and he gasps. He looks like he's seconds away from fainting.

My eyes flick down to the gun. He's too preoccupied with his bleeding eye to notice so I let go of Callie's hand and run to pick up the shotgun and Oliver's pocket knife. As I throw the knife back to Oliver, Callie runs forward and kicks Crud in the groin as hard as she can. He screams and falls to the floor.

"You bastard!" she shouts and kicks him in his stomach. Again and again. "You creepy son of a bitch! Kiss my foot! Kiss it!"

"Callie!" Jack grabs her arm and pulls her away, "That's enough! You're going to kill him!"

"Do you even know how to use that?" Oliver says, noticing the shotgun in my hands.

"It's not rocket science, Oliver," I say as I check if it's loaded. It is. "You just pull the trigger right? Plus, I've seen enough Walking Dead episodes to guess."

Oliver grins. "Alright then."

"Guys, c'mon," Jack says, tugging Callie down the path, "do you want to be sacrificed the great moon spirit above?"

We take off running through the last bit of the wooded path and out into the open space.

Chapter 13

Callie and I hop over the fence with ease - cheerleading for two years has its perks - whilst Jack and Oliver clamber up the fence. Oliver trips and falls unceremoniously onto the grassy floor. He curses as Jack helps him up and we sprint towards the house. Adrenaline pumps through me as I run in the narrow alley between the house and garage. Callie, Jack and Oliver quickly follow behind me. The front porch lights flicker on when we come to the driveway. I half-expect to see Flo Jo and Crud to be standing on the patio with shotguns but it's thankfully empty. The black SUV is parked a few feet away and we head straight for it.

"It won't open!" Oliver says as he rattles the handle of the car door. "Fuck! Where are the keys?"

Jack shuts his eyes for a second, opens them and then points to the house, "I saw Flo Jo drop them in a bowl in the living room when we came."

My mind moves at a million miles a second as I rattle through our options. "Okay, I'll go get them," I say, "You guys watch out for Flo Jo and Crud."

I turn and run up to the house. "Wait," Jack says.

I pause on the patio and glance back at him, "What?"

"I'm coming with you," he says, "Oliver look after Callie, we won't be long."

I open my mouth to protest but I don't want to waste time arguing so I just sigh and nod. If anything goes wrong I have the shotgun. Yeah, I don't exactly know how to use it but the sight alone should keep Flo Jo and Crud away right? I raise the gun as I open the door and we step into the darkened hallway. The floorboards creak and the spring wind sweeps in. Jack and I walk into the living room. As he starts searching for the keys, my eyes land on the vase Oliver broke. The pile of teeth are still there, I swallow and find myself hoping they're not human teeth again.

"Got them!" Jack said, jangling the car keys in his hands.

"Okay-"

A high-pitched scream pierces the air. Jack and I turn and run out of the house to find Callie and Oliver, they have their backs pressed against the cars. Callie spots us and points to the fence. Jack and I follow her finger and I gasp when I see the bear. It's standing by the fence, staring resolutely at Callie and Oliver.

"It's Patricia," Callie says.

"The fucking bitch followed us!" Oliver says, "Can you believe that? It's actually stalking us! Can this trip get any wierder?"

Callie hits his arm, "Don't call Winston's mother a bitch!"

"OW! She is a bitch!" he glares at her, "Damn it! You know what? I've had enough of your abuse, Callisto!"

For a moment we all just stand still, eying the bear and letting the bear eye us. Movement snaps into Jack as he tosses the keys to Oliver. Oliver just about manages to catch them. The bear growls and Callie screams. Oliver yanks the door open. He jumps into the driver's seat and Callie jumps in after him. A second passes before the engine roars to life but Jack and I are still standing on the patio having a stare down with the bear.

"Patricia!" Callie shouts next to Oliver, "Where's my baby? Where's Winston? You damn bitch! I trusted you! I....I loved you!"

"Now you're finally seeing the light, Callie!" He grins and then looks over at us. He leans out of the car window, "Hey! What the fuck are you waiting for? C'mon!"

Blood roars past my ears and I almost don't hear Jack. "Peryn," he says, "when I count to three, we run. Okay?"

I nod. The distance between us and the car has to be at least fifty metres. It's fine. We can do this. We have to. If we don't, well, I don't want to think about that.

"One," Jack says.

I swallow and my grip on the gun tightens.

"Two."

Patricia the bear is looking right at me now, baring its teeth like it's daring me to move.

"Three," he breathes, "Go!"

We jump off the patio and start running. Behind us the bear roars and leaps into action. It's now a terrifying race between us and the bear. It would almost be funny if we weren't about to die. The icy fear makes my heart and pumps my legs forward. I glance over at Jack, I'm a little bit ahead of him and my worry spills into fear.

Callie and Oliver are screaming at us, flailing their arms at us. Finally, finally, after what feels like forever, we reach the car. I yank the door of the back passenger seat open and hop in. I shove the shotgun into the corner and look back. I reach my hand out for Jack. I'm not sure if it's me or Callie and Oliver screaming his name but my throat feels raw from something. Jack grabs my hand and I pull him into the car. I fall back and he lands on top of me with a grunt.

"Go, Kaminski!" Callie shrieks, "Fucking go!"

The bear reaches the car just as Oliver drives off. Jack pushes himself off me and lies back on the seat. The car door is still open so he leans forward and slammed it shut. I sit up too and sigh.

We're breathing hard and fast as we look at each other. A beat passes and then we're both grinning so widely my mouth starts to ache. Jack brushes a hand through his dark hair and for some reason, the simple move makes my heart skip a beat. I take his hand in mine and intertwine our fingers together. Jack's grin softens into a warm smile as he lifts our joined hands and kisses the back of my hand. Heat coils in my stomach at the gesture.

"What the fuck?" Oliver says.

We look up and I gasp when I see Flo Jo standing in front of the large gate. She glares at us, shouting profanities as she waves her arms up and down. I glance at Oliver, his snaps his mouth shut and his jaw clenches as he scowls back at her.

"Oh you wanna play this game, you bitch?" He shouts and jolts the gear stick. "Okay, let's play!"

The needle on the odometer creeps up and up, from forty to eighty in two seconds.

"Oliver," I say, watching with baited breath as we speed straight to her. "Oliver, what are you doing?"

He doesn't answer, he just stares straight ahead. His knuckles whiten as his grip on the steering wheel tightens.

"Oliver!" I shout. Flo Jo is only metres away now.

At the last second, her eyes widen and she leaps out of the way. Oliver's face breaks out in a grin. Flo Jo has landed somewhere in the shrubbery. Callie, Jack and I look back, she pushes herself up and starts running after the car but its futile. We're going too fast.

"Oliver, the gate!" Jack says, "Watch out for--"

Oliver grits his teeth and rams the car straight into the gate. Metal screeches and the gates split apart as Oliver rams the car through. The crash leaves the gate wrecked and deformed in the darkness. Oliver keeps driving down the road, laughing as Callie whoops and claps her hands.

"Oliver Kaminski, I could kiss you right now!" Callie says, beaming at him.

Oliver laughs, "Hey, do whatever feels right."

My jaw is slack as I lean into the front of the car. "I seriously thought we were going to die but - oh my God, Oliver, that was amazing!"

"Thanks," He grins, "I've always wanted to do that...and I totally kicked ass at it."

Laughing, I lean back into my seat and look at Jack. The sudden paleness of his face makes my smile drop. "Jack?" I say, squeezing his hand, "What's wrong?"

He winces, "I think...I think the bear got me."

Callie whips back to look at us. Her eyebrows rise, "Got you? Got you where?"

He hoists his left leg up onto my lap and rolls his jeans up to reveal three bloody claw marks across his calf. Callie gasps as something twists in my stomach.

"When...when did this even happen?" I ask.

"Must have been when you were pulling me into the car," he says, "I felt something scratch me but in the rush, I thought I imagined it."

I peer at the cuts. "Okay, they don't seem too deep, we just need to..." I look around for a piece of cloth, just something to use but I see nothing. An idea pops into my head and I yank my crop top up and over my head. Jack's breathing hitches as he starts to splutter.

"Per-Peryn," he says with reddened cheeks and wide eyes, "what are you doing?"

I rip into the top until I have a long enough piece of cloth. I wrap it around the claw marks and tie it in a secure knot. I pat his leg and smile, "That should stop the bleeding for now but we really should take you to a hospital to get checked. I don't want it to get infected."

He slides his leg off my lap with a low wince and set its down.

"You didn't have to take your top off," he says and if it's possible, his face has gotten redder.

I laugh, "It's fine."

"Whoa, what? Peryn took her top off?" Oliver says and tries to look back but Callie punches his shoulder.

"Keep your eyes on the road, Kaminski," she says.

Oliver grumbles something about being oppressed by Callie Marshall but he doesn't turn around.

I can tell Jack is trying hard not to stare at my bra and it makes me want to laugh. He's seen me in my bra so many times (not that we've, y'know, done it, but our make out sessions would turn a little heated and one or both of us would end up topless before we cooled things off) and he always looks like he's going to combust each time. It's so cute.

He pulls his sweater off and hands it to me, "Here."

I smile when I see the white Avengers tee he's wearing underneath. I thank him and put the sweater on. It's a little too big for me and my heart races because it's warm and it smells like him. I didn't realise how much I missed wearing his clothes until now.

I look out of the window and I'm glad to find we're speeding down the highway, further and further away from that creepy couple. I hope we never see them again. We pass a neon sign that tells us Linbeach is only ten miles away. The radio comes on and Lana Del Rey's enchanting voice fills the air.

"Oh tell me I'm your national anthem!" Callie sings, rather terribly if I might say so, "tell me I'm your national anthem! Red, white, blues in the sky, summer's in the air and baby heavens in your eyes!"

Jack's hand finds mine again and I turn to him. Oliver groans and starts complaining about her terrible singing and Callie tells him to shut up or else. He doesn't, so they continue arguing like they always do but I'm not listening. I'm looking at Jack and he's looking back at me with so much candor and light and adoration it makes it hard to breathe.

"Are you okay?" he asks, his voice is deep and somber, sending shivers down my spine.

I can't help but smile and scoot closer to him. I rest my head on his chest. His heart is a drumming beat that showers me in this overwhelming feeling of home. He wraps an arm around me and I snuggle into him. I close my eyes.

"I'm great," I tell him.

Chapter 14

We reach Linbeach Hospital close to four in the morning. We would have gotten there earlier if Oliver hadn't taken directions from a drunk old man outside a bar. We drove around the same fountain in the town square four times before Oliver finally understands that yes, those directions the drunkard gave him were wrong. Luckily, we did spot a sign that lead straight to the hospital.

I'm guessing not much happens in the small town of Linbeach (population: 845) because when me, Callie, Jack and Oliver step into the hospital's lobby the receptionist eyes widen so much I'm afraid they're going to fall out. I admit we aren't in the best condition. Jack's limping from the bleeding claw marks on his leg, Callie still has this glazed look in her eyes like she's been smoking too much pot, I look really unhinged with my badly cut hair and Oliver is grinning at his pocket knife, flipping it up and down in his hands. We're battered and bruised and a little gaunt in our appearance but it doesn't justify the way she looks at us like we're demons as we approached the reception.

"Excuse me," I rest my hands on the desk, I don't miss how she flinches back a little. "We really need your help." I nudge my thumb to the right, to Jack, "my boyfriend's been attacked by Pat – by a bear, it cut his leg with its claws." Callie sighs and rests her head on the desk. I point to her, "And my friend here ate some toxic berries in the woods and she's been acting really weird ever since."

The uneasiness seems to seep out of her body when I offer her a smile but the worry is still there.

"Don't forget the drugging, Peryn," Oliver says, leaning back on the desk with his elbows.

"Oh yeah," I say, "and we were all drugged by some weird married couple who live about fifteen miles north of here."

"Weird is an understatement," Oliver says.

"How? How did this even happen to you guys?" she asks as she goes to pick up the phone, hopefully to call a doctor and not security.

I chuckle, "It's a long story."

"Right," she says, her brown eyes flickering between the four of us, "take a seat, someone will be with you in a second."

I nod, "Great, thank you."

We walk into the large waiting room opposite the reception. Callie quietly sings along to the One Direction song playing on the small speakers on the walls. We're not the only ones here, there's a middle-aged man in the corner. He's leaning forward with his elbows on his knees and his face in his hands. I'm just wondering what's wrong with the guy when Jack nudges me with his elbow.

"Hm?" I say, glancing at him.

He clears his throat, "Did...did you mean that earlier?"

"Mean what?" I say, even though I know exactly what he's talking about.

"When you said I was your boyfriend," he says, looking at me with those big brown eyes, "did you mean it?"

I answer him by leaning forward and pressing a soft, chaste kiss to his lips. "Of course," I whisper.

Jack grins.

Oliver makes gagging noises and we both give him the middle finger. Callie claps her hands. "Oh my God!" she beams, jumping up from her seat, "I knew it! I knew you two would work things out! You're, like, my OTP."

Oliver squints at her. "I'm sorry...your what?"

Before Callie can answer a doctor steps into the waiting room and walks over to us. The doctor is a spindly dark-skinned woman by the name of Dr Phillips who looks just as freaked out by us as the receptionist. She takes Callie and sends us off to different doctors. Apart from a few scratches and bruises Oliver and I are perfectly fine, although Oliver did try to milk it because his doctor was apparently "so hot he nearly died". The Marshall twins are another story. It turns out the cuts on Jack's legs will need stitches and the toxins from the berries Callie ate won't be out of her system for another nine hours or more, so they want to keep her overnight for observation. In some cases the Grenadine berries are known to poison the patient when they're in the bloodstream for over twenty-four hours and they want to be careful. They're also going to run some blood tests on us to check if there's anything else wrong.

I somehow manage to convince them to let the four of us stay in the same room together, so Dr Phillips sticks us in an empty six bed ward in the maternity department. To be honest the whole hospital feels a little empty tonight. Dr Phillips explains that the hospital is weirdly quiet on Thursdays. Not much happens in Linbeach. Apparently it's the healthiest town in the country, it's something to do with its practically non-existent crime rate and the fact there's no McDonalds or KFC anywhere in town.

"Don't you want to call your parents?" Dr Phillips asks us as we settle into our beds for the night. My nose crinkles at the smell of disinfectant in the air.

"Uh..." I say and we all glance at each other, wondering which one will have to make the dreaded call.

"Callie," Oliver says.

Jack and I nod in agreement.

Her face falls, "What? Why?"

Jack looks at her, stunned. How does she not get it at this point?

"Because this whole thing is your fault," I say.

She opens her mouth to protest but our glares stop her. She rolls her eyes and says, "Fine. I'll call my moms in the morning." She groans, "Oh my God, I'm so screwed."

The next morning, when Callie is tucked in her bed and Jack and I are sitting at the end, the police come into the ward and question us on what happened, on how we got to Linbeach, looking like we were half dead and a shot gun in the back of a stolen SUV. We tell the policewoman, a small redhead named Office Vygotsky, the whole story from getting lost on the highway and being chased by a bear to falling down a waterfall and being kidnapped by a creepy married couple called Flo Jo and Crud. I wouldn't believe it if it hadn't actually happened to me.

"Wait, Bosco?" Officer Vygotsky says at the end of our story. "Is he an overweight male in his late forties? He has a scruffy beard and wears a leather jacket that's way too small for him? Hitchhikes a lot? That Bosco?"

I nod, "Yeah, yeah, that one."

"That asshole stole my car," Callie says.

"Two days ago that very man was arrested about two miles from Linbeach for speeding," she says, "he'd been driving a blue Ford Fiesta that he later admitted wasn't his in the police station."

"Wait," Callie says with wide blue eyes, "So, where's my car?"

Vygotsky says, "Your car is currently being held at the local impound."

Callie squeaks and jumping off her bed, she gives the officer a tight hug. "Oh my God, thank you, thank you!"

Vygotsky has a sheepish smile on her face when Callie pulls away. She clears her throat, "You're, uhm, you're welcome."

"Is Bosco in prison then?" I ask.

"His trial's coming up next week," Vygotsky says, "he's looking at ten years in prison for Grand Theft Auto and burglary."

Callie and I grin. She turns to me and we slap our hands together in a high five. "Now that's what you call karma," I say.

"Just drop by the station in the next couple of days and I'll give you the documents you need to go collect your car at the local impound," Vygotsky says. She closes her notebook and tucks it into her breast pocket, "And don't worry, we've sent officers to Flo Jo and Crud's house. If your account is correct, they'll be arrested on sight."

I grimace slightly at the if in her sentence. Callie doesn't seem too concerned about it, she just smiles at the police-woman, "Great! Thank you, Officer!"

Vygotsky gives us a curt nod and leaves the ward. When I'm sure she's gone I turn to Jack and Callie and say, "Did you guys catch the if in her sentence?"

Callie blinks, "What do you mean?"

"Yeah," Jack nods but he seems as unperturbed by it as Callie, "It's okay, the police are going to get to the house and find the smashed gate, the poles and the weird teeth in their living room and anything else those creeps are hiding. There's no way they can cover all that up. Don't worry." He looks into my eyes and gives me a warm smile. "Everything's going to be okay."

It's only when he squeezes my hand that I visibly relax and smile back. "Yeah, you're right."

Suddenly, the long curtain that separates the beds is yanked to the side and the three of us jolt in surprise. For a horrible second I think it's Flo Jo and Crud, or even Patricia the Bear come back to finish us off but it's only Oliver. I sigh.

My eyes light up when I see the stack of pizza boxes in his arms. I don't think I've ever been so happy to see Oliver Kaminski.

He grins, "Which one of you bitches wants pizza?"

Callie gasps, "Oh my God, where did you get that?"

Oliver closes the curtain behind him and sets the pizzas down in the middle of the bed. "I convinced one of the nurses to let me order pizza from the Dominoes in town," he says.

"But how?" I ask, "I thought we weren't allowed deliveries in the ward?"

He smirks, "Oh, I have my ways, Peryn."

Jack's eyes narrow, "You cried didn't you?"

"Oh yeah," he chuckles, "I totally could have won an academy award for my monologue. She even paid for the pizzas man."

I'm about to scold him for tricking a poor nurse into buying us pizza when Callie opens a box and the smell of cheesy peperoni pizza causes my morals to go down the toilet. The poor nurse is pushed out of my mind as I grab a slice and take a bite. I almost start crying at just how delicious it is.

Oliver laughs at us. "Jesus," he grins, "you're acting like you've never tasted pizza in your life. Relax, you bunch of Neanderthals."

"Just...just shut up and eat," Callie says through a mouthful of pizza.

Since Jack and I are sitting together at the end of the bed, Callie scooches over and Oliver sits down next to her. They rest their backs on the headboard and I rest my legs over Jack's to make room for the cans of soda. Oliver chomps down on the pizza and lets out the most obscene noise that has us laughing our asses off.

"Who's the Neanderthal now?" Jack says.

"Shut up," he grumbles.

"Cal," I say, "did you call your moms?"

She holds one finger up as she chews and then swallows. "Oh yeah, first thing I did when I woke up this morning."

Jack cocks an eyebrow, "And?"

"And they're both really pissed, well Mom is pissed but Ma's just worried and confused," she says, "they're both driving up to Linbeach right now, they left about two hours ago, so they should be here in four hours."

Okay, so, it's not all bad. If it had been just Rosalie, we all would have been in serious trouble but with Luna, we'll be okay. We might just survive Rosalie's wrath and live to see another day.

"So, we have four hours of freedom and happiness before my moms get here," Jack says, he chuckles and glances at me. There's a soft smile on his lips. "I don't mind."

My heart hammers in my chest as he lifts his hand and wipes a splotch of tomato sauce off my mouth. His fingers graze the spot before he leans in kisses me soundly, long and deep and I can taste the pizza on his tongue. The kiss has butterflies swooping in my stomach.

When we break apart, Jack's cheeks are flushed and his lips are red and he looks as intoxicated as I feel. On the other side of the bed, Oliver starts making yet more gagging noises. Jack and I half-heartedly glare at him as we go back to eating our pizzas.

Callie punches his shoulder and he cries in pain. "Shut up, Kaminski, you ruined the moment."

"Stop abusing me!" he scowls at her as he rubs his arm.

She scoffs, "Well, stop being a dick."

"I'm the dick?" he says.

"Yes, you're the dick!"

Oliver gasps, "Oh my God. You're so fucking deluded, Callie! How the hell am I the dick?"

I smile at their antics and when I look over at Jack I see he's just as amused.

"So," Jack says, taking another bite of his pizza, "who wants to go camping next week? I heard it's pretty fun."

Oliver and Callie stop arguing and give him the most incredulous look, like he's lost his mind. I burst out laughing and almost choke on my pizza. Jack rubs circles into my back as I cough. He grins at me, wide and brilliant and I grin back.

And so here I am, sitting on a hospital bed with these morons, tired and bruised from days of running in the woods and you know what? I wouldn't want to be anywhere else.

Epilogue

3 MONTHS LATER

James Wolfe Secondary School, Vancouver

Fourth period Spanish on a Tuesday makes me want to gouge my eyes out. I'm starting to understand why Mrs Roderick was punched in the face by those actors last Christmas. She's talking about – about something or another, I think it's to do with conjugating verbs into the future tense but my mind is drifting off.

It's the last week of school and then it's summer vacation. The whole school is buzzing at the prospect of two whole months off. This summer's already looking pretty good. Callum, my older brother, is coming back from military school in early July and then we're going to Jamaica for two weeks to visit our grandparents. It'll be great to spend some time with my brother. Since he's been at military school, I've only seen him a couple of times a year. Summer vacation means no more six a.m. wake up calls, no more Spanish with Mrs

Roderick, just no more school for two months. Praise the lord.

I don't really wanna think about how fast junior year went or about senior year (and ew, college applications and exams and just no). You think you're going to spend an eternity at school but something happens to remind you that it's going to end someday.

"Psst!" Oliver hisses, yanking me out of my thoughts, "Psst! Peryn!"

I turn around in my seat to look back at Oliver Kaminski. He likes to sit at the back in every lesson so he can catch up on the sleep he lost from band practice the night before and play games on his cellphone. When he's not sleeping or on his phone, Oliver likes to mess with Mrs. Roderick by correcting her Spanish or asking inane questions with the most serious expression. It's entertaining and it does kill time but it's also the reason I'm failing this class. It would be alarming but my GPA's holding up pretty well. And anyways, there's always senior year. I'll have to ask Callie (who's surprisingly good at Spanish) or Santiago Garcia to tutor me. Jack says that I need to average a B in Spanish if I want a good GPA score.

I raise an eyebrow at Oliver. I whisper, "Yeah, what?"

Oliver brushes his dark hair back and leans forward in his seat. "So, what did Ruby say?"

I fight the urge to laugh out loud. Callie's right. He's so in love with her.

"She says she'll come," I tell him.

His hazel eyes light up as he grins brightly at me. "Seriously?"

I smile, "Yeah, so you better not screw it up."

Friday is the last day of school and Oliver's parents are out of town so he's throwing an end of year party. He's already convinced some of the seniors to bring kegs. Words gotten round and everybody's anticipating it to be the biggest party of the year. They don't know that Oliver's only throwing it so he can finally make a move on my cousin, Ruby Blakewood. Callie has been counting down the days until his party for two weeks now. Honestly, I think she just likes any reason to dance on tables.

"Yes!" he hisses, "Thanks Per."

"You're still gonna play right?" I ask.

I told Ruby that Oliver's the lead singer in a band (weirdly named Fat Monkey Heart) and she's really looking forward to watching him perform at the party.

"Oh yeah," he grins, "but do you think –"

"Oliver! Peryn!" Mrs. Roderick snaps at us. "Pay attention!"

I jump slightly in my seat and turn to the front. She's glaring at the both of us, and I can tell by the look in her eye that she's looking forward to not seeing us at all over summer. I just hope we don't have her next year for Spanish.

"Sorry, miss," Oliver offers a flashy grin that I know will only infuriate her. "It won't happen again."

Her eyes narrow even further and I think she's going to issue us a detention but she just sighs and goes back to the board. The last twenty minutes of the lesson go by painstakingly slow and when the bell finally rings, I let out an audible sigh. Everyone shoots out of their seats and practically races out of the room.

"We might only have one more lesson left before summer break but I want everyone to have finished reading El Sur by Jorge Luis Borges!" she shouts as we all shoot out of our seats and head for the door. "Have your notes ready because we'll be discussing it tomorrow!"

I suppress a groan. It's a short story but the thing is written in Spanish. Why did she have to add Spanish literature to this class? As if it isn't hard enough. I can barely string a sentence together let alone read an entire story. I take comfort in the fact there's one more period left then it's home time.

"Enjoy gym," Oliver snickers as we leave the class.

"Enjoy detention," I say.

Yesterday, in second period Chemistry, Oliver somehow managed to set Mr. Sokoloff's toupee on fire during a lab experiment. He claims he saw a bug in his hair and that he was only trying to get it off for him. So, Oliver now has detention every day afterschool for the next week. If he shuts his mouth and stays out of trouble until the last day, he won't have to go to summer school. Oliver huffs and he heads down the opposite end of the corridor. I watch him go for a moment, wishing that I could be in Study Hall with him and Jack instead of P.E with the likes of Jude Sinclair and Reinette Thayer.

Life after the whole camping disaster is still the same but better somehow. As I predicted Mom totally freaked out when she found out what had happened. I left out the parts about being chased by wolves and nearly sacrificed to some moon spirit so she didn't die of a heart attack. I just played the wounded daughter card and I avoided two hours' worth of lecturing from my parents.

Callie and Jack were grounded for two weeks by their moms. Callie's only recently got her car back since Rosalie confiscated it for almost three months as a punishment for being so careless. Oliver got off scott free with his parents, he played the wounded son card and his mom has been treating him like a lost prince ever since.

After nearly twenty years of marriage, Mom and Dad renewed their wedding vows last month. It was a beautiful but small ceremony near English Bay Beach. The planning was stressful and Mom had me tearing my hair out from all the nagging but it was worth it in the end. It was worth seeing her smile and the look on Dad's face when she was walking down the aisle. They flew my brother over from his military school in New Hampshire for the weekend for it and even though Mom knew he was coming, she still squealed like Christmas had come early and almost crushed him in a hug. It totally beat Drew Barrymore's wedding by a milestone.

I turn and make my way to P.E. I walk into the girls' locker room, it's filled with the sound of chatter and everyone is already getting undressed. Ruby has just disappeared into the toilets to get changed since she's never liked getting undressed in public. Callie, on the other hand, is standing in the middle of the locker room in just her bra and panties. Ammara looks distressed as Callie wiggles her ass in front of her face.

"Callie," I say as I drop my bag on the long bench between the walls of lockers, "What are you doing?"

She stops dancing and says, "I'm trying to show Ammara that I'm a better twerker than Miley Cyrus."

"She's not," Ammara says.

I pick up Callie's P.E top and chuck it at her, "Get dressed, this isn't a strip club."

"I would be such a good stripper," she says, almost wistfully as she pulls the white polo on.

I open up my bag and take out my kit.

"Totally," Ammara nods, "Hey, y'know, Reinette Thayer told me the strip club in Burnaby is hiring, you should try it out!"

I laugh as I take off my clothes and start pulling on the school's standard P.E uniform, which is just a white top and black shorts.

"Hey, say what you want about strippers but some of them make a shitload of money," Callie says.

Ruby gets out of the toilet and I feel a twinge of envy at the sight of her long hair. It falls down to her elbows and sways as she walks over to the wide mirror in the back. Even though my hair nearly reaches my shoulders since it was cut by Flo and Crud three months ago, it's not long as it used to be and it probably won't be for another year or two. Ruby bunches up her black hair into a messy ponytail and rests her hands on her hips.

"Is Callie talking about being a stripper again?" she asks.

Ammara chuckles, "Yep."

"So," I ask as I sit down next to Ammara on the bench and start pulling on my sneakers. "What's everyone's plan for the summer?"

"Per and I got jobs at the Public Library for the summer," Callie says, looking way too smug. "The pay's descent and the hours aren't too long. We start in two weeks, it's gonna be so fun, me and Per checking out all the cute college boys –"

"You will be, I won't," I tell her, "I have a boyfriend."

"Doesn't mean you can't check them out Per," she says, "Like, I'm taking a break from guys but I can still appreciate them from afar."

I don't even know how Callie managed to get us jobs at the Public Library as part-time assistants but I'm not about to look a gift horse in the mouth. God knows I need the money. I don't want the beat-up mustang Dad used to own when he was in college, I wanna save up for a decent car. Something like Callie's, new, modest but easy on the eyes. Of course, that it's if I pass my driving test. Which is coming up in mid-August and I'm dreading it but Jack keeps reassuring me that I'm going to be fine.

I glance at Ammara, "What about you? What are you doing this summer?"

She shrugs, "Nothing much, probably just go to work at my uncle's pharmacy or go see my cousins in Colorado like we do every summer."

I know Oliver's going to be cooped up in his garage doing nothing but band practice for the next two months. And, Jack, well he says he's going to be preparing for senior year by studying and looking over the course material but I know for a fact he's just going to end up playing video games and arguing with his friends over the latest issue of Young Avengers. No one's summer sounds particularly glam this year but I don't think anyone cares.

"What are you doing this summer, Rubes?" Callie asks, tucking loose strands of blonde hair behind her ear. "Sleep," Ruby says with a sigh, "Sleep for two months straight. This school is killing me. Before this, I had Geography with Mr. Kanagawa and it was terrible. The guy couldn't teach theology to a priest."

"And making out with Oliver Kaminski," Ammara adds with a knowing smirk.

If it wasn't for Ruby's brown skin, a shade darker than me and Ammara, her face would be bright red. I laugh as she tries to sputter a response but I can tell that the idea of making out with Oliver is really enticing.

"You need to make your move at his party on Friday," Callie says, "I swear you two aren't together by the beginning of twelfth grade I'm going to punch someone."

There's a hint of a smile on her lips. "You guys sure he likes me?"

"Ruby, the guy has been crushing on you for two years," I say, "Trust me, we're sure."

The smile Ruby gives us is so blinding, I can see why Oliver is so infatuated with her.

"Don't worry," Ammara say, "we'll make sure you look really hot and he won't be able to resist."

Callie and I nod in agreement. Once I've finished tying up the shoelaces of my white converses, I half-heartedly leave the locker room with the girls. We go down a brief corridor and step out onto the sports pitch. It's hot and the sunshine is pounding as we join the rest of the class. Jack and Oliver are lucky, their last period on a Tuesday is Study Hall. So whilst we're sweating our asses off in P.E, they get to sit in an air conditioned room and relax. I know Oliver certainly doesn't do any work, Jack tells me he likes to throw wads of paper at Mr. Bardet when he's not looking.

"Alright class, let's play some baseball!" Mr. Osmond shouts, his voice echoes through the field and birds scatter from their trees.

"Oh God," Ruby groans. Ruby Blakewood objects to any form of exercise, if she was brave enough she'd probably skip P.E with Oliver. She still thinks me, Callie and Ammara are crazy for joining the cheerleading squad.

"Listen up!" Mr. Osmond says, instantaneously silencing every single student, "Sinclair and Rosenberg are the team captains! So, they're going to be picking their teams!"

"Ew," Callie says as Jude Sinclair flashes everyone a grin. It's safe to say Callie Marshall has lost all and any interest she ever had in Jude Sinclair. I think the camping trip finally made her realise just how much of a douchebag he is and I couldn't be happier for her.

Jude points to the redhead near the bleachers. "Reinette."

She smiles and walks over to him, a shit-eating grin on her face. It's Ethan Rosenberg's turn and no one is really surprised when he picks his boyfriend first. Santiago comes to stand next to him, he smiles and bumps their shoulders together. Jude picks Tyler Wright next, who is actually a good choice since he's the best player on the varsity baseball team. I high five Callie and Ruby when they end up with me on Ethan's team.

Ammara isn't so lucky. I can tell by the way Jude's blue eyes linger on her that he's going to pick her. "Ammara," he says.

Ammara's eyes widen and for a moment, I think she's going to run away but the look on Mr. Osmond's face stops her. She groans and stalks over to him. Our team gets to bat first. I spot Ammara standing by the third base, looking rather unimpressed with her arms folded over her stomach.

I'm pretty lame at baseball, so it's no surprise that I miss the ball and barely even make it to the second base before I'm out. Santiago laughs at me, "That was so bad, Peryn, oh my God."

I roll my eyes, and slump down onto the soft grass. The cool shade cast by the oak tree is a welcome haven from the sun. "Whatever, at least, now I get to chill."

Ethan runs past the last base and our team cheers for him. Callie grabs the bat from him and hops onto the home plate with an excited squeal. Jude smirks at her, "Hey, babe."

"Bite me," she says with an intense glare in her blue eyes.

Jude just laughs and throws the ball. Callie swings too early and misses the ball but the bat slips from her hands and spins straight ahead. Right into Jude's crotch. He squeaks and everybody gasps. You can see the colour drain from his face as his knees buckle and he falls to the floor. One second, we're all frozen, and the next the whole class has crowded around him. Jude writhes on the floor, cupping his groin as he lets out a stream of curses, a high majority aimed at Callie.

I cover my mouth to stop myself from cackling. I'm shaking with laughter as I watch Jude roll around on the floor. Callie doesn't care, she's bent over and laughing as loudly as she can.

"Callie, it's not funny," Ammara says but she's grinning.

"Step away!" Mr. Osmond shouts as he pushes his way through the class. "Jude! Jude, can you hear me? Jude, are you OK?"

He doesn't answer; he just keeps groaning.

"Take that as a no then," Ruby mumbles.

"Callie!" Mr. Osmond calls.

"Yeah?" She says.

"Since you're the one who hurt him, you can be the one to take him to the nurse's office."

Callie's laughter dies, "No. It was an accident, I didn't mean to hit him!"

Santiago and Ethan help lift him. Callie sighs. They step aside so she can wrap an arm around his waist.

"Oh God, my crotch is on fire," he whispers as he slings his arm over her shoulder.

Callie chuckles, "Yeah, well, that's what you get for being an asshole."

I watch as Callie and Jude head over to the main building.

Mr. Osmond blows the whistle, "We have time for a few more rounds, let's go!"

Ethan walks past us and hands the bat over to Ruby, "It's your turn Blakewood."

"No," Ruby groans, "No, please."

I look at her and smile. "Oh, cheer up, Rubes," I say, "it could be worse, we could be stalked by a crazy bear or sacrificed to the great moon spirit above."

Ruby and Ammara shoot me confused looks.

"What?" Ammara says.

I laugh again and shake my head, "Nothing."

I say goodbye to Ruby and Ammara. They both have rehearsals for the school play the drama club is organising so they won't be going home for another two hours. Ammara really regrets letting Ruby sign her up for the play but it's too late to back out now. The play is on Thursday and she's got one of the main roles. Jack's waiting for me in the courtyard when I finish P.E. He's sitting on one of the circular tables, earphones in as he flicks through a thick textbook. I skip down the steps of the main building and walk over to him. He looks up just as I'm about to tap his shoulder. The sunlight catches his eyes, bringing out the flecks of golds in his irises. He pulls out his earphones and grins.

"What you reading?" I ask, gesturing to the open textbook in his hands.

"AP Computer Science," he says, "Miss Booth's set us so much work for the summer, not to mention she wants me to enter in the national science competition."

"National science competition?" I say, "well, obviously, you should...You have all these great ideas for computer programs and even though I don't understand any of them, I know they're brilliant. Just think about how good it would look on your college application if you entered."

"I might not win."

"You're the smartest person I know," I say matter-of-factly, "You're amazing...of course you'll win."

A small smile graces his lips as he looks at me, his gaze is piercing. "Peryn."

My heartbeat picks up. I let out a soft chuckle, "What?"

He shuts the textbook and slides off the table. I stare at him, my eyebrows knitted together in confusion as he steps closer. He slides a hand behind my neck and tugs me forward for a kiss. My eyes flutter shut and I wrap my arms around his neck. Jack's smiling into the kiss and I can't help but let out a breathy laugh and tug him closer. Kissing Jack always makes me feel light and heady like I'm going to float off into space any second. I half-expect Oliver to be making gagging noises when we break apart but then I remember he's in detention for setting a teacher's toupee on fire and I laugh.

Jack gives me a dazed smile. He takes a step back so he can shove the textbook in his rucksack and shrugs it on his back. "Where's Callie?" he asks.

"She hit Jude in the crotch with a bat and Mr. Osmond made her take him to the nurse's office," I say, "She won't be out for another hour, apparently Jude's making a big fuss about it."

He laughs, "Seriously?"

"It was so good, I wish I'd taken picture to show you, he looked like he was gonna cry," I grin, "So, do you wanna take the bus or walk?"

Callie was supposed to drive us but she's stuck in the nurse's office with Jude.

"It's a nice day," he says, glancing up at the clear azure sky and then back at me. He takes a hold of my hand and locks our fingers together. "Let's walk."

Jack finally convinced me to start watching Game of Thrones, so we're going back to his place to watch a couple of episodes. If I like it, Jack says we can marathon the first two seasons on the weekend, which sounds pretty intense but I'm not objecting to spending the weekend in his bedroom. Jack's place isn't too far, it's only thirty minutes on foot and plus, it really is a nice day. When Oliver finishes his detention, he's gonna come over and watch Game of Thrones with us. He's already seen it but he says it's too sick of a show not to re-watch, especially with a newbie like me. I have a feeling Callie's going to join as well but if it's as gruesome as Oliver says it, she won't last twenty minutes.

Jack and I leave the court yard hand in hand and walk past the parking lot, where Ethan Rosenberg and Santiago Garcia are not so subtly making out against Ethan's car. It makes me smile.

"Get a room!" I shout.

They jump apart, probably afraid it's a teacher or Luke Kinder and his asshole friends but when their eyes land on me and Jack a few cars away, they seem to relax. Santiago cards a hand through his already mussed up dark hair and laughs.

"Oh, we're about to!" Ethan shouts back. He presses a brief kiss to Santiago's lips and walks around the car to the driver's seat.

"See you guys tomorrow," Santiago says. He throws us a grin and hops into the car with Ethan. Ethan backs his car out of the parking space and drives off into the main road out of sight. We walk through the car park and out of the school grounds. The thought of coming back to James Wolfe tomorrow is a little depressing but knowing we only have three days left until summer vacation is keeping me going.

Jack squeezes my hand and says, "Hey, you wanna stop by that new ice cream shop on West Broadway?"

"Hell yeah," I grin at him, "If I ever say no to that question, I want you to punch me."

"Ah, I don't know about the punching but I can manage a really lame push?"

I laugh as we cross the street, "Deal."

www.ingramcontent.com/pod-product-compliance
Lightning Source LLC
Chambersburg PA
CBHW071827190726
48292CB00005B/1640